# CHRISTMAS PRESENCE

## Haunted Everly After
### BOOK THREE

## REGINA WELLING
## ERIN LYNN

# Christmas Presence

ISBN- 978- 1703162592

Cover design by: L. Vryhof

Interior design by: L. Vryhof

http://reginawelling.com

http://erinlynnwrites.com

First Edition

Printed in the U.S.A.

# Contents

# CHAPTER 1

"Everly!" A woman's voice came at me like a bullet when I stepped onto the porch. "Mrs. Hastings, your husband is under investigation for funneling restricted funds back into the family business. Was it your idea or his?"

Molly, my otherwise-friendly chocolate lab, growled and bared her teeth. I'd have done the same thing if there hadn't been a news camera pointed my way. I could just see the headlines from that one:

Feral Former Philanthropist Frightens Photographer

On the plus side, with my winter hat pulled down over my forehead and the collar of my puffy jacket tipped up against the cold, the camera wouldn't pick up much of a reaction shot. Plus, I wasn't sure if I was annoyed or happy that the station had sent their perkiest on-air personality out for the interview. That meant they didn't think I was headline news—which I didn't want to be anyway, but if you're going to do a thing, do it all the way is my motto.

"Mrs. Hastings," she prompted, and I dragged her name out of memory. Amber Hale. With a name like that, she should have become a meteorologist. One of those perky ones who make a blizzard sound like fun. She even looked the part with her upturned nose, bow-shaped mouth, and shiny blond hair sleeked back into a neat little twist at her nape.

I opened my mouth to answer just as Patrea Heard pulled up behind the news van. For once, my attorney didn't look like she'd just rolled off the showroom floor. She wasn't wearing any makeup, and her hair, cut shorter since the last time I'd seen her, ruffled up along the center part. Even messy, I liked the new style; it flattered an interesting face.

Patrea's hair was not what I should be thinking about while standing on my front steps in the freezing cold when my dog had to pee, but there you go. The mind settles where it will when confronted with the unexpected. Or the partially unexpected in this case.

"Don't say a word," she warned me in a hoarse echo of her normal tone. "*Miss Dupree* has no comment to make at this or any other time." Patrea emphasized my newly-single status, and maiden name.

"*Miss Dupree*," Amber corrected herself, somehow managing to keep her camera face on while giving the impression of an eye roll, "would be wise to take this situation seriously. Officially divorced or not, she worked in a position of authority during the period when the funds were mismanaged. That, combined with the timing of the separation brings into question Miss Dupree's involvement. She's going to have to tell her story at some point."

She pointed the microphone in my direction, and the scruffy-looking guy with the camera took another step closer to my front porch. Molly let out another grunt that did nothing to break Amber's confidence.

"Go back inside, Everly." Molly would have to settle for a romp through the backyard snow drifts in place of our afternoon walk because Patrea brooked no refusal. I didn't get to hear what she said to the reporters because Molly danced around me with that look on her face, so I headed for the back door.

Four months had passed since Patrea warned me that my ex-husband's family might come under legal scrutiny for the dispersal of not-for-profit funds I had raised for them before my divorce. During those four months, my divorce had finalized, and I managed to convince myself I was finished with Paul and his family for good. I try not to make a habit out of being wrong, but it just keeps happening.

2

"Give it to me straight," I followed Molly in from the back of the house. "How much trouble am I in?"

As Patrea stripped off her ankle-length wool coat, I nearly fell over in shock. Underneath, she wore an ancient looking sweatshirt and a pair of pajama pants.

"You're sick." Stating the obvious is one of my strong suits.

Her *I'm fine* sounded more like *I'b fibe* because of a stuffy nose. She pulled out a travel pack of tissues, honked a few times, cleared her throat, and managed to speak above a croak. "You've got me on your side, and if I'm half as good as I think I am, you have nothing to worry about. But you have to do exactly as I tell you. No talking to the press. Not even about the local Christmas pageant. And try not to find another body. The last thing we need is your face plastered all over the TV in connection with another untimely death."

"We're not having a Christmas pageant," I ignored the untimely death comment.

Patrea raised her left eyebrow, tilted her head slightly to the right, and stared at me.

"Fine. We're having a town-wide lighting contest."

"I knew it had to be something. It's like a sickness." Speaking of sickness, Patrea sneezed hard enough I thought her shoes might blow off, then moaned and clutched her head.

"Come sit." I didn't have to ask twice. Patrea followed me into the living room and practically collapsed on the sofa. "I've got some stuff you can take for that cold."

"This is not a cold. It's the plague, and it laughs in the face of modern medicine."

"Then I guess it's a good thing I have other options." I put on a pot of water to heat for tea and dug through my medicine cabinet for Leandra Wade's cold and flu remedies. My best friend's mother had a flair for natural healing. When I returned, my patient had removed her boots and was huddled under the knitted throw I kept on the back of the couch.

"Take this." I poured a spoonful of darkly red syrup.

3

Shivering, Patrea gave the spoon a sniff. "What is it?" She tried to hand it back to me.

"Elderberry syrup. Just take it."

She did, and when she shivered again, it wasn't from feeling cold. "It's got a kick to it. Burns all the way down."

"I think it's half moonshine, but it works. Now," I took the spoon back and motioned for her to hold out her hand. When she did, I produced a bottle and shook two shiny beads into her hand. "This is an essential oil blend to boost your immune system. Don't look at me like that. I know how it sounds, but my best friend's mother gets these for me, and the oils really do help. Just let the beads melt on your tongue while I make the tea." Since I had the bottle out already, and Leandra swore they were good for preventing illness, I shook out another two for myself to fend off Patrea's germs.

If looks could kill, I'd have been the next body found in Mooselick River, but Patrea went ahead and popped the beads into her mouth. She might scoff, but Leandra's remedies were as good as gold. I heard muttering from the living room while I scooped dried echinacea into a strainer ball, and a gasp of surprise when the gel encasing the essential oils burst in Patrea's mouth. I'd grown used to the intense flavors of citrus and cinnamon.

A squeeze of lemon, and a dash of honey in the tea, and it was ready to drink.

"What's in the cup? Eye of newt, toe of frog, wool of bat?"

I rolled my eyes at her. "No, it's herbal tea. When was the last time you had anything to eat?"

"Why?" She frowned.

"Because I thought you might be hungry."

She blew on her tea to cool it, and considered. "Not really. What day is it?"

"Thursday."

"Thursday?" She put a hand to her head. "I started feeling nasty on Monday, went to work on Tuesday to finish up

4

before my vacation, but had to leave early, and I must have slept through Wednesday."

I had to ask. "How did you manage to drive all the way out here if you don't even know what day it is?"

"Painkillers and adrenaline, I suppose. Both of which have now worn off. I feel like a wrung-out dishrag."

"You don't even look that good."

Wrinkling her nose at me, Patrea also offered a rude hand gesture. I wondered if she had anyone at home to take care of her, and tried to remember if we'd ever had a conversation about her relationship status.

"Why don't you stay here tonight? I've more than enough room, and you shouldn't be driving when you're this sick." Besides, taking care of her would give me something to do other than worry about Paul's next move. I hadn't spoken to my ex since the day I caught him in bed with another woman, and yet, he was one ghost from my past who refused to stay in the grave.

Patrea drained her cup, then handed it back to me. "I'll be fine. Just let me sleep for an hour or so, and I can drive home." So saying, she snuggled back under the throw and closed her eyes.

Imagine me saying this in an ominous narrator voice: Patrea would not, in fact, drive home that day.

# CHAPTER 2

On her third day with me, Patrea made her shaky way down the stairs to the sound of the doorbell ringing followed by the hammering of a fist on the frame.

"Aren't you going to get that?" she asked.

I snorted. "It's Amber Hale again. She has some sort of mental block against the word no."

"You haven't talked to her, have you?" Weak as a kitten, Patrea couldn't muster up even a shadow of her usual stern face.

"No. She shows up here like clockwork three times a day, and I ignore her." It didn't seem like a good idea to admit I sometimes yelled through the door for Amber to go away. "Are you sure that's the best way to handle things? Seems to me that the longer I go without making a statement, the more it looks like I have something to hide."

To confirm my thought, Amber shouted my name through the glass. "Everly Dupree. Open up. You're not doing yourself any favors here. Just answer one question and I'll go away."

Annoyed, I shouted back, "The answer is yes, I do find you highly annoying, are you happy now?" To Patrea I said, "She's wearing me down."

Patrea waved off the arm I offered her, and made her way to the kitchen unaided. A definite sign of improvement.

"Feed me something with substance—anything that isn't chicken soup—then I'll take a shower, and we'll figure out our next move." Another good sign, as was the hint of normal color in her cheeks after days of fever pink.

Over poached eggs and toast, Patrea asked to be brought up to date.

"There's nothing much to tell. The family closed ranks with a blanket statement of no comment funneled through their attorney in the matter. One thing I found interesting is they're not using Winston for this."

"Well, he's an idiot, and he's probably in it up to his eyeballs." With each bite of solid food, Patrea's voice gained a bit more volume and strength. "If I drink the rest of my tea like a good girl, can I please have a cup of coffee? Hot and strong enough to strip the paint off the floor."

Because her eyes were clear, and she hadn't coughed since she'd come downstairs, I went ahead and made her a pot. She hummed over the first sip, then took another. "You're probably right. It's time to address the rumors. Toss the ball right back in Paul's lap and tell the press you're willing to cooperate fully with the authorities."

"Of course, I am. Aren't I? I mean, not that they've shown up on my doorstep. Don't you think that's odd? I don't really know anything that would help, but it seems like someone would at least ask some questions."

"They'll get to you, and when they do, you need to let me do the talking. The investigation is in the preliminary stages right now, which is why Amber's here on a major fishing expedition. She's got nothing, and we're going to give her more of the same, but it doesn't hurt to knock the family off balance a little."

"Whatever you think is best. If she holds true to form, Amber will be back at one which gives us," I checked the clock on the wall, "three hours to get camera ready."

Patrea looked down at herself ruefully. She wore one of my nightgowns, and by the fit, it was clear that none of my clothes would do the trick. "That gives us enough time to get to my place and back if we leave soon."

"I take it you didn't open the blinds before you came downstairs." I'd been keeping her room as dark as possible so she could sleep. "It's been snowing since this morning. The storm has already dropped three inches of wet stuff, and it's supposed to turn to sleet by noon. The roads are a mess. Even with four-wheel drive, it's going to take longer than we have."

"Ugh!" Patrea clapped a hand over her right eye because it had begun to twitch. "It's important that we look confident. How am I supposed to pull that off in my pajamas?"

I did not snort, but only because I bit the inside of my mouth to hold it back. "We don't have a lot of choices in town. The tackle shop stocks jeans and flannel shirts."

"I can't decide if that's a step up or down."

Only one other option presented itself. "How do you feel about vintage? You're about the same height and weight as the woman who owned this place before me. She left behind this gorgeous, two-piece suit from the 1940s. Fawn-colored jacket with a cinched waist over a pencil skirt. Think Casablanca."

The suit was gorgeous enough I'd been tempted to have it altered to fit me. Instead, it was on consignment at Curated Collections, the new store owned by my best friends, Jacy and Neena. "It's a classy suit, and it beats going on TV in your jammies."

Patrea slugged the last of her coffee, and shrugged. "Or looking like I spent the morning trolling for the catch of the day. Show me."

By the time she showered, the weather report had changed. But then, Maine weather tends to defy prediction. Instead of the promised sleet, heavy snow continued to fall in sheets and swirls.

"Here," Patrea handed her keys to me. "You drive." The short walk through drifted snow to her car proved she wasn't entirely over her illness. Later, I decided, I would insist she stay at least one more night.

With the lousy weather, I wasn't even sure the shop would be open, but Jacy and Neena insisted I keep a spare key in case one of them lost theirs, and they wouldn't mind if I went in for the suit. When we pulled up, I noted in surprise that not only were both women working, but there were even a couple of customers browsing around.

"People are flat crazy," Patrea muttered on our way in. "Why would anyone be out in this weather?"

"We're out."

"Shut up." There was no heat to the order, and I couldn't hold back a smirk.

By the time I introduced Patrea to my friends and pulled the suit off the rack for her to try on, the store had emptied out.

"How's Peanut?" I studied Jacy's face.

Jacy rested a hand on her belly where the baby bump seemed to grow larger every time I saw her. "Kicking up a storm." She glowed. "I think Peanut is practicing to become a kick dancer."

"You keep Peanut all stirred up is why." Neena shook her head. "I can't get her to be still for a minute. You've known her forever, is there some kind of trick to settle this woman down? She's like a butterfly, just flitting from one thing to another all day."

"That's a load of lies. I sit plenty." To prove it, Jacy perched on a barstool behind the counter. "See."

Neena rolled her eyes, but didn't get to voice her rebuttal because Patrea exited the changing room looking moderately pleased.

"This isn't half bad, you know. The tailoring is exquisite."

As always, Jacy had a kind word. "Well, it fits like it was made for you, and you look very authoritative."

"It does," I agreed. "Crisis averted."

"Crisis?" Neena and Jacy said at the same time.

"Amber Hale has been ringing my doorbell three times a day over this mess with Paul. Now that Patrea's feeling better, we decided it's time to give her a statement. But there was the

9

slight problem of the weather, and Patrea not having anything to wear on camera. I remembered this suit was still here, so crisis averted."

Excited, Jacy jumped off the stool, and started to say something when Neena cut her off.

"See what I mean? Three minutes and she's back up and moving. Makes me tired."

But the comment did what it was meant to do, and Jacy sat back down. "Fine. I'll sit, but I have gossip about Amber Hale."

Patrea pulled the price tag off the suit, handed it to Neena, and motioned for her to ring up the purchase. "Gossip? Do tell."

"Well," Jacy said, "Amber and Darcy Campbell got into a huge fight at the grocery store yesterday. I wasn't there, but everyone at the diner was talking about it. They were really going at each other. Darcy slapped Amber across the face. Amber kicked her in the shins. There was a scuffle and then Ernie broke the whole thing up, is what I heard."

"Over what?" I asked. "Did Darcy bump Amber with a grocery cart? Or was Amber trying to get through while she hogged the aisle?" Both could send my blood pressure up the charts.

"I'm not sure if anyone heard how it started. But the name-calling and hair-pulling—that's been confirmed from several sources."

Her eye having been caught by a glass-fronted hutch, Patrea wandered off for a closer look. Over her shoulder, she said, "Amber should be more careful. Getting into fights with strange women isn't the best way to stay on the air."

"Who said they were strangers? Amber is cousins with Darcy's husband and she'd been staying with them since she showed up in town. The station tried to call her back, but she didn't go. That's the rumor, anyway."

"Maybe," I said, "she took some time off to visit for Christmas."

"I don't think so, the big van with the satellite doodad on the top is gone, but Ginny Rollins told me there's a car with the channel numbers on it at the Bide-A-Way. We figured they left her a camera person."

Neena gave Jacy a big grin as Patrea ran a hand over the polished wood and tested the hutch drawers to see how well they opened and closed. I could have told her they worked flawlessly since it was one of the many pieces of furniture I'd found in the back rooms of my house.

Anticipating a sale, Jacy grinned back, but kept up her end of the conversation. "Well, Amber and Darcy don't seem to get along very well for being family. Or family-in-law, as the case may be."

Neena huffed out a breath. "Don't get me started on in-law stories. I've got a few for the books."

Married to my other ex, my high school sweetheart until his untimely death, Neena had the misfortune of landing Viola Montayne as a mother-in-law. When Hudson had been murdered right after I moved back to town, Viola blamed his death on me, and then took out the rest of her ire on Neena. The woman was poison on a stick.

"Anyway," Jacy said, "I don't think that's why because according to my sources, Amber moved into the Bide-A-Way yesterday. Why wouldn't she just go visit her father if she had time off? I think he lives in Hackinaw."

"Big mystery in a small town." Patrea smiled to take away the sting of sarcasm. "Do you deliver?"

"Within fifty miles, sure. For a fee." Neena's returning smile was genuine, but her eyes had gone sharp with the prospect of a good dicker.

Numbers flew back and forth like a ping-pong ball until the two women struck a deal. I didn't know which one got the better end of it, but both of them looked happy when Neena handed over her credit card.

11

# CHAPTER 3

Back at my place, Molly tilted her head and watched me rush to get ready in time for Amber to ring my doorbell, and then we waited.

And waited.

Amber never showed. Not for her midday attempt or her after dinner one. It looked like she wasn't coming at all.

As the hours passed, Patrea's face lost color except for flares of pink on her cheeks. "You're trembling again, and your eyes are too bright. I think you're having a relapse." Ignoring her protests, I fed her, made another pot of tea, and dosed her with more elderberry syrup. She looked better after, but not by much.

"I'm fine. As soon as it stops snowing, I'll get out of your hair. I've imposed on you long enough. If Amber shows up tomorrow, you know what to say."

It was my turn to burn her with a look. "Did anyone say you were an imposition? I've been avoiding asking certain questions because it didn't seem right to pry, but to hell with that. Do you have family waiting for you? Or someone who'll look after you while you recover? What about work? I haven't heard your phone ring once the whole time you've been here."

I didn't know if she'd speak or snarl, but Patrea gave me a ghost of a grin. "Not exactly, and I always close the office from Dec 15th until the first of the year. This year I guess I closed on the 12th because I was too sick to work."

"What you're saying is I'm the one who's imposing on you, then—interrupting your vacation."

She shook her head. "Not you. Your idiot ex and his shenanigans couldn't wait a few more weeks."

"Amounts to the same, doesn't it? You wouldn't have risen from your sick bed to come all the way out here if not for me."

Patrea waved away my concerns. "If I'd been on my game, I could have quashed the story with a phone call. It's my own fault for turning off the ringer for a few hours. But the donor who made the allegations made them months ago, and it seemed like the whole thing had blown over until it blew up instead."

I'd thought the same thing.

"What does *not exactly* mean?"

"It means my folks decided to take a cruise to someplace warm. My sister and her husband are spending the holidays with his folks, and since I'm not seeing anyone at the moment, I'm at loose ends. I thought I'd decompress with a few boxes of ribbon candy and a DVR full of Hallmark movies. Maybe check out some of the holiday sales at my favorite antiques stores. You get the best prices once tourist season is over."

"Wait there." I went to the kitchen and returned with a candy box. "I have this, and my DVR is overflowing with romance under the mistletoe. Why don't you stay?"

I like to think the ribbon candy won her over, but it was probably the still-falling snow, and the lingering fever that had Patrea convinced. "One more night."

"No. Stay through the holidays. Have Christmas here. It'll be fun." The woman had offered to defend me pro bono if it came to that, I couldn't let her spend the holidays alone. Besides, if she got comfortable enough, she might tell me what beef she had against the Hastings family that warranted going to the mat for me even if I couldn't afford to pay her.

"Christmas in a small town," she considered. "If you're sure."

"I am. It'll be fun," I promised. "You can live out your very own Christmas movie adventure."

13

"Pass me the box, Everly. And kick on the TV."

We'd set aside the candy in favor of an eclectic meal made from leftovers and were right at the part where the heroine's car broke down on the outskirts of town and the hunky man in a tow truck pulled up alongside when my doorbell rang.

"I can't imagine that's Amber at this time of night," I said. It had stopped snowing, but the roads were still slick.

"Well, if it is, she's out of luck. Tell her to come back tomorrow."

Reva McKinnon, the woman who waited on the other side of the wavy glass was worse than Amber. Way worse.

"What are you doing here, Reva? Haven't you caused me enough trouble?"

Fury rose up to swamp the first stab of pain at the sight of her face, and I whipped open the door to snarl at her. "Get off my porch."

"I know you don't want to see me, and I don't blame you, but we need to talk."

"No, Reva, we really don't. There's nothing you can say to me now that I care to hear, and I won't demean myself by using the kind of language I'd need to tell you what I think of you. Go away."

When I tried to close the door, she stuck her foot in the way so I couldn't. "We were friends once. I hoped that would be enough to let you hear me out."

"Friends?" Heat stole over my skin, starting with my neck and creeping up toward my hairline. "Friends don't sleep with each other's husbands. We were nothing remotely close to friends, and now you're nothing to me but another lie."

"I never meant to hurt you. At least hear me out. You owe me that much."

I closed my eyes, took a deep breath, and let the image of planting my fist in her face wash over me like a happy memory. The desire to turn the fantasy into action was so real to me I could almost hear it breathing. When I opened them

14

again, I let the expression in them go dead. "I owe you? That's rich."

"Don't be an idiot." Patrea stepped up behind me. "The best way to deal with liars and cheats is to let them talk until they reveal their true motives."

"Who are you, and what do you know about anything?" Reva snapped.

I had to admit, Patrea made sense. There was more on the line than my emotions, and so, I grabbed my coat from the hook and stepped onto the porch, not quite closing the door behind me so she could hear everything Reva said.

"Say what you came to say, but you're not coming inside." The betraying skank wouldn't sully my home any more than she had already. The twinkling lights around the door cast flickers of color over her skin, and I couldn't help it, I searched her face for the person I'd thought I could trust, but that woman was dead to me now.

"You need to leave Paul alone."

At first, I couldn't process the words because they made no sense. At least not in that order.

"What?"

"Leave him alone. We're trying to move on, make a life for ourselves, but he can't if you won't let him go."

Was she out of her ever-loving mind?

"Listen, I don't know what he's told you, but I haven't seen, spoken to, or attempted to contact Paul since the day I found you in my bed. I'd have preferred to keep it that way with you, too. You're dead to me. Both of you. Why won't you rest in peace?"

In a flash, Reva's face went from earnest to crafty. "He's not going to pay you another dime, you know."

I wanted to tear out my own hair. No, that's a lie, I really wanted to tear out Reva's. Every last bottle-dark strand. "Another dime?" I couldn't stop the laugh that shot up from out of nowhere, or the one that followed it. Now, it was Reva's turn to look at me like I'd lost my marbles.

15

"Oh, that's rich. Another dime." I was overcome with another fit of the giggles and, maybe underneath them, a little hysteria besides. "You're deluded, you know that? I'd almost feel sorry for you if I didn't despise you so much."

Apparently, I wasn't giving Reva the satisfaction she'd expected to find because she hauled back a hand and slapped me across the face. That was a mistake.

Growling and spitting, Molly shot through the cracked-open door like a sleek, brown bullet. Reva let out a squeak of terror, and raced for the steps. I'm not proud of it, but I let Molly take Reva down before I grabbed my dog's collar and pulled back hard.

Scrambling to her feet, Reva shouted, "I'm calling the police, they'll take that dog away and put it down."

"Go ahead and try it." My cheek still burned from the print of her hand. "And while you've got him on the phone, tell Ernie I want to file assault charges against you."

As I knew she would, Reva backed down.

"Listen closely, Reva, and nod if you understand the words that are coming out of my mouth. Paul is a liar and a cheat. You should know this about him since those are traits you have in common. Whatever he's told you, he hasn't given me *one* dime much less another. I wouldn't take his tainted money in any case. The man steals from the homeless. Think about that when you climb between those four hundred-dollar sheets he likes so much. And don't forget, I'm the one who picked them out."

"You'll pay for this," Reva slipped a little on her way back to her car, but I suppose that's what you get for wearing screw-me heels in the middle of winter.

"Oh, trust me honey, I already did."

Turning my back, I said to Molly, "Come on girl, let's get you a treat, you deserve one," then stalked inside and slammed the door.

Patrea clapped me on the back and practically chortled. "That was priceless."

"I'm glad my discomfort amuses you." The fire in my veins still burned, and wanted fuel.

"Come on, you know I didn't mean it like that. That parting line, though. Let's get you a treat for knocking that piece of trash on her ass. Remind me never to get on your bad side."

The corner of my mouth twitched. Just a little. "I shouldn't feel like laughing after a confrontation like that, but the look on her face when all Molly did was stand on her. That image will stay burned into my brain forever."

"Well, sweet little Molly has the heart of a lion and she looked like hell on four paws going down those steps."

I got the dog a treat and gave her a couple of extras for being so protective. Patrea and I discussed possible reasons why Reva would show up on my doorstep at this particular time, and since we'd never have the truth, went back to our movie before any more ghosts from my past decided to visit.

# CHAPTER 4

"Where's Brian? I thought last night was his late night to work," I said when Jacy showed up at the lighting contest alone. Under a red-and-white knitted hat, her blue eyes sparkled. "Someone called in and he jumped at the chance for the extra overtime before we close on the new house, so I figured I'd come waddle around and look at the lights by myself. Who do you think will win?"

"You realize they can probably see this town from space." Bundled up in her long wool coat over a pair of the jeans she'd had to break down and buy from the bait shop, Patrea half-smiled to take the sting from the statement.

"And all it took," I said, "was a fifty-dollar value gift from every business in town to make it happen."

"Hey, we were happy to donate our share." Neena wore no hat, only a scarf pulled up around her neck, and a band to cover her ears. A riot of curly hair framed her face. "The publicity you generated would have cost us ten times that at least. The shop's been hoppin' all week."

"I can't take too much credit for this one. This contest has been running since I was a kid. I only suggested taking the prize and advertising up a notch."

Except that in Mooselick River, if Martha Tipton was involved, one notch was more like ten. Honestly, though, the town looked amazing in its holiday finery. Anything that stood still for more than five minutes ended up with a string of lights stuck on it. The town even coughed up the funds for two dozen sets of solar powered lights for the welcome sign, the town monument, and anyplace else where outlets were too far away to run extension cords.

Pine swags, also lighted, adorned lamp posts and light poles, which had been wrapped in candy cane red-and-white bands. The high school marching band stood ready to launch into a spirited rendition of Santa Clause is Coming to Town, and the jolly elf himself—played by none other than my boss, Leo Hanson—was slated to arrive in a horse drawn carriage within the next ten minutes.

As we slipped behind the crowd waiting for his arrival, Patrea and I shared a grin when we heard someone say, "This is better than a Hallmark movie."

I worried she might be a little shaky still, but after a good night's sleep and a couple of decent meals she seemed much stronger.

"This way!" Jacy grabbed my arm and pulled me toward the narrow access between two buildings that spilled into the parking lot behind her shop. "I cordoned off the steps so we'd have the perfect place to watch the spectacle from." She hustled us through the shop and out the front door just in time to hear the band strike up the first notes.

Next year, she'd watch for Santa with a baby in her arms. I didn't begrudge Jacy her burgeoning family—that's not my style at all—but I did envy her a little. This latest business with Paul only solidified my decision never to get tangled up with another man. Ever.

When it came to men, I wasn't comfortable trusting my own judgment. I'd laughed when my mother warned me about Paul, but she'd been right. To make it worse, I'd moved back home and spent several weeks treating David—the son of my father's close friend—a fine and decent man, with enough disrespect that I was still ashamed of myself. Granted, he'd moved in with my parents and I thought he might be taking advantage of them, but that was no excuse for my behavior.

I'd have to settle for being the best aunt I could be to however many babies Jacy and Brian decided to have, because one of my own was off the table.

Santa arrived and, after waving and hamming it up for the crowd, took a seat to listen to the children's Christmas wishes. Judging by the length of the line, he'd be at it until the lighting contest judges counted the votes and announced a winner.

"Who are you betting on for the win?" Jacy asked while we warmed up inside the shop for a few minutes before hitting the far end of town. "I've got ten bucks on Viola Montayne. Sorry Neena."

Neena rolled her eyes. "Oh, she'll win all right. She's weighing heavily on the pity factor. Did you hear she hired some guy to recreate Hudson's face in lights on her roof? It's tacky, that's what it is. My poor Hudson would be mortified if he knew."

"I guess it's a good thing he's not hanging around and haunting the place." Jacy nudged me in the ribs. I'd had to tell her about my spate of hauntings when she almost became the next victim of murder.

"Oh, I don't believe in ghosts, even if my granny claimed she could see her dead husband right up until the day she died."

"What about you, Everly?" To my utter shock, Patrea seemed genuinely curious, "Any ghosts roaming around your place?"

"Not at the moment." I told the truth. "I'd like to keep it that way."

I should learn to keep my big mouth shut.

Warm, and ready to buck the crowd, we headed back out the way we had come in. I didn't notice the others had stopped to wait for Jacy to visit the restroom, so I kept going. Outside alone, I heard half of a phone conversation from somewhere close.

*No. I was here on time, but she never showed.*

20

*Yeah, I checked her room, and I called her cell, but she's not picking up.*

*If you hear from her, call me. It's not like Amber to flake out on a story.*

*No, I haven't sent the footage yet. Data's iffy here, so I'll have to use the satellite link...*

The man's voice faded as he left the area, and I turned back in time to see Patrea coming up behind me.

"They're bickering over a display like an old married couple."

"They do that a lot. It doesn't mean anything."

My point was made when, all smiles, Jacy locked the back door behind her, twined her arm around Neena's, and stepped out into the frosty air.

"Let's go gawk at Hudson's face in lights," she said. "No disrespect intended. Unless seeing him immortalized like that would be too painful, because if it is, we'd completely understand."

"If I said yes," Neena bumped Jacy with her hip, "You know you'd only go back later and look, and then I'd have to wonder forever what you saw."

Neena pegged it. Now that I knew what Viola Montayne had done, I really wanted to see, and I was sure Jacy felt the same. "Not if it bothers you, though. You're more important to me than satisfying a burning curiosity."

"No, it's okay." It was too dark to see if there were shadows in Neena's eyes, but her tone sounded okay to me, "I need to see for myself. People are going to be talking about it for years to come. Besides, I don't want to hide my Hudson away, seeing his photos on the wall brings comfort. Talking about him isn't always easy, but not talking about him makes it seem as if I'm trying to forget him, and I'm not. My life was on track and headed in one direction until Hudson died, and now I'm over here in this new place and it's going somewhere else. I can't go back there because where I was is gone, and it doesn't do to dwell in the past. I can only pick myself up and move forward from where I am now."

Since Jacy was closest, she was the one to pull Neena in for a hug.

"That might be the most profound thing I've ever heard anyone say," Patrea's voice and tone were gentler than any I'd ever heard her use before. Sooner rather than later, I intended to pry her story out of her.

"Hudson was a good man. He loved you and he'd want you to be happy." His ghost had assured me of that before he left, so I had it on good authority.

Neena's eyes might be misty, but her smile said more. "He'd want me to climb up on his mother's roof and take his face down off of there, is what he'd want."

"Hey," Jacy said, "I know a couple of his friends who would do it for you for a case of beer. Probably for a six-pack."

"It's a thought."

As we chatted, we strolled past the diner and toward the first of the residential streets on that side of town. Viola and her husband lived three blocks over on Maple. Taking our time, we twined through Oak and Elm—the area known as the tree streets—looking at all the lights.

"I think this is my favorite so far." Jacy stopped beside a picket fence outlined in pink and purple lights. More of the same colors mixed with off-white decorated a pair of evergreen shrubs flanking the walkway. "Look how they wrapped the tree trunks so tightly. It must have taken hours and a big ladder to go that high. Makes the trees look like torches. It's lovely."

She'd have stood there longer, but Neena dragged her away. "I like Santa's workshop over here, and they're handing out candy canes. Let's get one."

"You know that's a blatant bid for votes, right?" I said.

All attendees were allowed one vote in the lighting contest. Anyone wishing to vote could visit Martha and her

22

cronies at the booth set up near Santa's chair and pick up a token—one per person. Voters were encouraged to look at all of the entries and drop their token in the box in front of the home they liked the best. It was a simple system, and not exactly foolproof since there was no way to stop family members from voting for their own.

Based on the reactions of people coming back from the Montayne house, we knew we were in for an experience. Some grinned, some whispered with their companions, some just shook their heads. Then again, that was the reaction Viola had on people most of the time anyway.

Still, as prepared as I thought I was, I stood open-mouthed when I got my first look.

"When they said his face in lights," Jacy said in a stage whisper, "I figured they meant something like one of those wire reindeer figures you put on your front lawn."

"That would have been creepy enough, but this is just...it's—" Patrea waved a hand to indicate words had failed her at the sight. It must have cost Viola a fortune to have her son's likeness programmed onto a digital billboard and mounted on her roof.

"It's downright hilarious is what it is." Neena snorted, and then she started to laugh. Deep, rolling belly laughs that soon had her doubled over, holding her sides and gasping.

"Should we slap her out of it?" Jacy wanted to know. "Isn't that what you do when someone goes off the deep end?"

I couldn't decide how to feel about the whole thing, but I didn't think Neena needed to be punished for finding it amusing. "Let her be."

"No, she's right." Neena wheezed, "I don't think I can stop."

"Well, I'm not slapping you, so you'd better get hold of yourself," I said.

The front door opened and Viola spilled out onto the steps. "You think this is funny?" She slurred her words. "My

23

Hudson was worth more than all of you put together." She waved her arms wildly around her head.

Neena sobered up. "No, Mother Montayne. It's not funny." She approached the steps like one might when facing a cornered animal. "I miss him, too."

A small crowd had gathered, but now most people decided they had somewhere else to be and cleared out quickly. Well, except for Jacy, Patrea, and me since we weren't about to leave Neena alone with Viola.

"You shouldn't be here." Viola sounded like a wounded child and I wondered where her husband was while his wife stood in the cold with no coat or hat. "I don't want you here."

"Oh, I know you don't," Neena said, and then she proved whey Hudson had fallen for her. "But I'm here, and I loved him, too." She took off her coat, wrapped it around her mother-in-law, then wrapped arms around the older woman as well. "I still do."

Viola stiffened for a moment, and I worried Neena might end up being slapped after all, but then all the fight went out of Viola and her arms went around Neena.

"That right there is your Christmas miracle. I guess you can chalk that off your small-town holiday wish list," I said to Patrea.

While Neena helped Viola inside and got her settled, Jacy and gave Patrea a history lesson. Jacy got a little misty-eyed in the process, but put the excess of emotion down to being pregnant. Still, she admitted, "I almost want Viola to win the contest now."

When Neena returned, she seemed lighter in spirit than she'd been for months. "I've been invited to spend Christmas with the in-laws. If Viola remembers this tomorrow, anyway."

Brilliant lights against fresh snow, happy children making ooh and aah sounds, families being healed. It just didn't get better than this.

24

"You know," Patrea echoed my sentiments, "I thought Christmas in the boonies would be boring, but this is actually nice. I almost want to make a snow angel."

I cocked an eyebrow at her because the mental image of the buttoned-up attorney flopped over in the snow was one for the books.

Jacy clapped her hands, the sound muffled by thick mittens. "We should all do that. Come on, it'll be fun." Now the idea was in Jacy's head, it would take a nuclear attack to dislodge it. "Let's find a spot right here in town so everyone can see them in the morning."

Easier said than done. Between tracks made to install lights at the last minute and people wandering everywhere, finding a pristine stretch of snow large enough for four full grown women to sprawl out in turned out to be more difficult than expected. We finally ended up in front of the only building in town that wasn't lit up for Christmas: the law offices of Josiah Caldwell.

"This is the perfect spot," Jacy decided. "Let's give the old Scrooge something to look at in the morning."

So saying, she climbed up on the snowbank, spread her arms wide, and took the backwards plunge. A soft whumping sound rose as she landed. Not to be outdone, Neena chose a spot near Jacy while Patrea and I made our mark on the other side of the walkway. Two or three inches of fluffier snow over the top of the heavier, wetter stuff made for perfect snow angel conditions.

Only a little chill seeped through my clothes and reddened the tip of my nose as I arced my arms and legs with graceful, simple pleasure, then scrambled up to see the results of my efforts.

"Um, I could use a little help here." Pregnant belly in the way, Jacy was having trouble with her snow angel dismount. Laughing, Neena extended a hand, but it took both of us to get our friend back on her feet.

Dusting snow off Jacy's back, Patrea nearly giggled. "You looked like a beached whale in a Santa hat." That I'd never heard her sound so lighthearted meant she'd needed this time among new friends and made me wonder if she had a group like this back home.

Before I could ask, the smile fell off her face to be replaced by a frown, and her gaze moved past Jacy to something beyond the pool of brightness made by the streetlight. When she moved toward whatever it was she'd seen, I followed behind.

"What's wrong?" I asked.

"Do you see that?" She pointed to a snow-covered hump. One end seemed to be lit from within.

Not for the first time, a sense of otherworldly dread washed over me. Something wasn't right here.

Ahead of me, Patrea pulled her phone out of her pocket and activated the flashlight setting.

"That's one of those solar doohickeys." Jacy had her phone out as well, and was looking toward a spot sheltered from falling snow by the roof overhang. "The wires are buried, but the collector part isn't, so the lights are still working even though there's a bunch of snow on top of them."

She hadn't yet realized the shape of the snow hump resembled a person lying prone. Patrea had, and her eyes met mine. I nodded, and we began to paw through fluffy white to uncover what was underneath.

"Go back out front, Neena. Take Jacy with you, and call Ernie Polk," I said. I guess the third time is the charm, because I didn't throw anything or scream when we uncovered Amber Hale's lifeless face. "Tell him to hurry, though I suppose there's no need for it, now."

Of course, Jacy didn't go willingly, but once she got a glimpse over my shoulder, she couldn't get away fast enough. I'd have like to follow her, but someone needed to stay with the body and I wasn't going to leave Patrea to handle the onerous task alone.

26

"Strangled," Patrea announced. "With Christmas lights. How very festive." Her dry tone was back.

"Now we know why she didn't show up yesterday."

"Didn't I tell you not to find another body? The last thing you need is more of this kind of publicity."

There was a sentence I never expected to hear. "Technically, I didn't. You found her, so don't try and blame this on me." I almost regretted talking Patrea into staying for Christmas. She'd brought along the ghosts of my past, called into question the ghosts of my future, and unless my luck had taken a turn, set me up for a ghost in my present.

# CHAPTER 5

"Everly Dupree." Ernie greeted me with a look of inevitability on his face. "You know, I can't remember the last time there was an incident and you weren't there. You carry a black cat and a broken mirror around in your pocket?" Already on crowd control, he arrived on foot.

I held my hands up in surrender. "Hey, I'm just a bystander this time. Patrea found Amber Hale's body. Looks like she was murdered."

Without answering or moving anything other than his eyes, Ernie took in our snow angel handiwork, and I swear I saw his lips quirk just a little. My face grew hot, but I introduced Patrea and told Ernie how we'd come to be there. Something jingled in the belt around his ample waist when he followed us to the scene of the crime.

"Strangled." Using the beam of a high-powered flashlight, Ernie looked at the body and echoed Patrea's earlier comment. "With Christmas lights. Merry fricking Christmas."

Bypassing dispatch—most likely to keep Carol Ann Wilmette from spreading the news far and wide—Ernie called the death in to the county coroner's office, and we gave our statements while he waited.

"I think you'll find she went missing sometime yesterday between ten am and one pm." I tried to be as helpful as I could.

"You just told me you didn't know the woman personally, so how could you possibly be able to pin her death to a three-hour timespan?"

28

In order to explain, I incurred Patrea's wrath by telling him about the trouble with Paul's family.

When she poked me with an elbow, I turned on her. "What? I didn't do anything wrong, and I can't begin to see how any of this connects to the death of a woman I don't even know. Well, other than that she'd established a pattern of knocking on my door that changed yesterday. If I can help Ernie figure out who killed her, I will—including airing my dirty laundry to him. It's not like he's going to go talk about it on the five o'clock news."

Patrea huffed out an exasperated breath. "You can't know that."

"Yes, I can. Ernie's a good cop and a stand-up guy who does the right thing even when it hurts him personally. I trust him."

Despite the seeming animosity between us I felt bad for Ernie, but he was a decent man right down to the ground. Because of me, a few months earlier he'd had to arrest his sister for murder and two counts of attempted murder.

"If you're done dissecting and assessing my character, I'd like to get back to work. You ladies are free to go. I'll be in touch if I need to ask more questions."

"I'm half frozen." Neena shivered, probably not entirely from the cold. "Give me a ride home?" Neena lived right across the street from me.

"Sure. What about you?" I turned to Jacy. "You're not walking, are you?"

Shaking her head, Jacy said, "No. I'm driving. My ankles swell sometimes, so I figured I'd take it easy on them."

"Okay. Text me when you're home and safe. We'll do the same." I gave her a hug. "Where are you parked? We'll walk you to your car."

"Brian will be home by now. I'm parked around the corner." Finding Jacy's car, even at the edge of the circle of streetlight, wasn't hard. The color stood out.

29

Her voice as dry as the sun, Patrea observed, "That's a whole lot of pink."

When the little plus mark on the stick turned blue, Jacy had decided it was time to trade in her baby for something more appropriate for a woman about to have one. The hot pink Jeep with the candy-striped top had gone to a good home and would make another teenage girl a fine first vehicle.

Cash in hand, Jacy had put a down payment on a slightly used mini-van in a silvery gray color. She managed to drive it for a solid week before begging her father-in-law for a new paint job. You had to give her husband Brian credit for having the stones to be seen driving around in her signature color, because on a minivan it was, as Patrea had pointed out, a whole lot of pink.

"Wait until you see the seat covers, I found, but I'm not going to tell you about them now and spoil the surprise."

We waited until she pulled out and watched her taillights turn the corner toward home before walking the half block to where we'd left Patrea's car. No one talked about the dead woman. I think because it was too much to take in all at once.

"Are you okay to go in alone?" I asked when Neena hesitated a moment before getting out of the car after we'd pulled up in front of her place. The drive had been too short to get the heat going and I was ready to get out of my damp clothes, but I'd go in with her if it helped.

"Yeah, yeah. I'm fine. Security system's on. It's just seeing that woman just lyin' there all still and cold—made me think of what it must have been like for you when you found my Hudson."

Leaning forward, she gave my shoulder a squeeze. I rested my hand on hers, returned the favor, but this was one of those times when I'm never sure of the right thing to say.

"You're welcome to come over and hang out with us for a while if you don't want to be alone."

"Thanks, sugar, but I'm all churned up and the best thing for me is to channel all that emotion into my work. The easel is callin' my name."

"Sensible woman," Patrea said once the car door shut behind Neena. "You should take a page from her book and get a security system installed at your place."

"Why? Mooselick River's a safe place to live." I realized the absurdity of the statement at about the same time she gave me her *stop talking BS* look. "Okay, so maybe it used to be safer and things have changed a little."

The admission did nothing to take that look off her face. I'd been attacked twice. Once in my own home, and then again tracking down my boss's killer, but that didn't mean anything.

"Besides, I have Molly."

Molly had belonged to my former boss, and I'd sort of inherited her after he died. She was young yet, a chocolate lab with a keen interest in chasing tennis balls and knocking over my peonies in the summer. She greeted us with her dance of welcome when we walked in, then dropped to the floor to sprawl on her back in case a belly rub was in order.

"Yeah, she's a killer." Along with her health, Patrea's sarcasm had returned.

"Hey, you saw what happened with Reva. Don't discount Molly. She has a keen sense of people, and she's usually right. Speaking of which, she growled at Amber Hale right before you showed up the other day. I'm betting she sensed there was something off about the woman."

"She could have been growling at the guy with the camera."

"No, she was growling at me."

I'd hoped, since I'd made it all the way home un-haunted, that somehow, this time would be different. But no, Amber faded in behind Patrea. Molly promptly let out a rumbling growl.

31

"See," Patrea almost shouted in triumph. "I've been here for days, and she never made a peep. You can't trust that dog's judgment."

It is not polite to argue with house guests, and I really wanted her to go upstairs and change into dry clothes to give me a minute or two alone with Amber

"Maybe you're right." I kept my eyes on Amber's face. "It's still early enough to flip on the DVR and take our minds off of tragedy." When she looked unconvinced, I added, "You can jeer at the hopeless Christmas romantics."

When she said she had planned to eat ribbon candy and watch a slew of feel-good holiday movies, I expected to see the softer side of Patrea. I should have known better.

She could make fun of ingénues all night if it got the topic of murder off the plate. "But I can't eat another bite of ribbon candy. I'm making popcorn after I let Molly out and get changed."

"I could eat some popcorn, and I wouldn't mind the distraction." Her tone turned wistful. "It's too bad something had to mar what was otherwise a really decent evening."

Wisely silent up until that point, Amber muttered, "Excuse me for being an inconvenience. What about a little compassion, huh?"

I kept my expression neutral while internally face-palming and regretting my decision to invite Patrea stay for the holidays. At this point, my only saving grace would be if Ernie found Amber's murderer before I slipped up and said something to her ghost at the wrong time.

As soon as Patrea's door shut behind her, Amber hit me with the question. "Did you know what your husband was doing with those restricted funds?"

I parried her question with a whispered one of my own. "You're dead. You know that, right?"

"Of course, I do. I watched you dig me out of the snow, didn't I? Just answer the question, Everly. I'm dying to know."

32

Damn, I hoped she didn't mean that literally. Moving past her, I headed for my room to put on something dry.

"Why aren't you begging me to find your killer? Threatening to haunt me forever if I don't." That's how these things usually worked.

Amber shot me a feral grin. "Waste of time. I'm here, you don't want me here, you'll do whatever it takes to get rid of me. Threatening you would be pointless, so put me out of my misery and tell me what you know."

The old dresser drawer made a ratcheting sound when I yanked the drawer open to select my oldest, most comfortable pair of flannel pants and a warm sweatshirt.

"I'm going into the bathroom to change. Don't follow me. That's the first rule if you want my help."

Her lips twisting into a snide smile, Amber waved a hand at me. "Such a prude. No wonder Paul Hastings dumped you."

"Listen, I know it's considered impolite to speak ill of people who no longer breathe, but you really are a piece of work. It's probably what got you dead. Think about that for a minute, and when I come back out, we'll talk about the rules you'll follow if you want me to look for your killer."

Amber shrugged, and managed to look completely unconcerned.

While I changed, I realized I had an ace in the hole.

"You want to know about the Hastings family, and I want your time with me to go smoothly. It's in your best interests to cooperate, so here's what I expect from you. Respect my privacy. That means you don't talk to me when other people are around, and you don't pop into the bathroom with me or watch me while I'm sleeping."

"Why would I want to do that?"

"I don't know, the last two ghosts were men."

"Okay," she laughed. "Done. Now, spill some details."
She wasn't going to be happy to learn I didn't have any.

"I'm not finished. There's one other thing. Whatever it is that lets me see you—it's not something that I have any control over. You're haunting me, which, if you ask me, is presumptuous and rude, so don't expect me to pass along your heartfelt goodbyes to your family. I won't be sending messages to anyone on your behalf. You want to tell your mother you're sorry for being an insensitive brat, go find a medium."

Impatient, she waved a hand in the hurry up gesture. "No messages to family, got it. When did you find out your ex-husband was diverting charity funds back into the family business?"

A prickle of energy ran along my arms, lifted the hairs and raised goosebumps. If Amber realized her heightened emotions could affect the physical world, she'd be impossible, so I rushed to diffuse the situation.

"My job was to raise funds. I was good at it, too. But I didn't have anything to do with how those funds were dispersed. When the checks came in, they went to the accounting department, not to me."

Amber looked disgusted. "So you were nothing more than a glorified party planner."

I bristled at the description, but didn't correct her. If she thought of me that way, she might be more likely to let the subject drop.

"Pretty much. I have to go now, I have company. We'll talk more about this later. In the meantime, you need to start putting together a list of the people who might have wanted you dead." With her attitude, the list was probably long.

# CHAPTER 6

Over popcorn and candy cane-sweet TV romance, Patrea and I discussed possible motives for Amber's death, but having so little information about her we ran out of steam fairly quickly.

In fact, Patrea ran out of steam entirely before the first movie ended. After her recent illness, the events of the evening had taken a toll.

"Are you feeling okay? Any congestion? Or fever?" I searched her face for signs.

"Just tired. I sincerely hope I don't see Amber's face in my sleep." The mighty Patrea shuddered at the thought.

"The first time's the worst." Seriously, how ridiculous was that comment?

"I'm counting on this being the only time, and I'll thank you to keep your body-finding cooties to yourself."

Because death was no laughing matter, I bit down on the giggle that wanted to surface at Patrea's use of the word cooties, and snorted instead. "It's more of a wrong place, wrong time sort of thing, but I take your point."

When she'd gone upstairs, I puttered around with cleaning up and getting Molly settled for the night. We had a moment of growling when she saw Amber sprawled over the bed, but then the dog tilted her head to the right and stopped. After a head tilt to the left, she went to her bed, circled a few times and slumped over to sleep.

There wasn't time to think about odd canine behavior.

"What can you tell me about your death?" I wanted to order her off of my grandmother's quilt, but I settled in the chair at the desk I'd converted into a space for my jewelry and makeup instead.

"About as much as you've told me about your ex, which is precious little, I might add. I don't know who killed me because they came up from behind. Now it's your turn. Tit for tat. What happened between you and Paul?"

Even if I didn't want to talk about it, who was she going to tell?

"He cheated, I left." Two could play the brief answer game. "Why were you at Josiah Caldwell's office? Were you in some kind of legal trouble?"

"Family business. Not pertinent," she snapped. I'd touched a nerve. "Were you fired or did you quit your job when you left?"

Now I was the one who winced. "They let me go. Were you working on anything else while you were here?"

"Just that stupid lighting contest."

Since I didn't kill her, and I couldn't see a connection to the lighting contest that was worth dying for, we were at square one for establishing a motive. Until she glanced around the room, sneered, and asked her next question.

"Is this place the best you could do with your divorce settlement?"

"I didn't get a divorce settlement," I said in a clipped tone.

"Prenup?"

She saw the answer in my eyes.

"Idiot."

"Just remember you're the one who's dead and needs my help finding your killer. It's probably not a good idea to piss me off." I couldn't help lashing out, but I guess it was the correct response because Amber sat up and assessed me with interest.

36

"So there *is* a little fire under all that meek and mild. Good, you're going to need it before this is all over."

My stomach dropped. "What are you talking about?" Tit for tat went out the window.

"I don't know if they'll still run it now that I'm...you know, but I did an interview with Paul Hastings where he implied you were the one skimming funds and that he filed for divorce the minute he found out. I came here to get your side of the story, but your lawyer friend showed up and put the kibosh to my plan."

If Amber wanted fire, she was about to get a bigger taste of mine. Okay, so it was a little banked because I was keeping my voice low so Patrea wouldn't hear, but for the first time since the beginning of my marriage debacle, fury rose up to eat me whole. With nothing else to hand, I took out my wrath on an errant makeup sponge that was laying out loose, and shredded it with vicious twists of my fingers.

"Dirty, rotten sleaze-weasel. Lying piece of—"

My tirade had gone on a while, and apparently, I'd been less quiet than I thought because Patrea banged on the door and asked what was wrong.

On the bed, Amber laughed herself silly. "I'm dying," she said. "That idiot has no idea who you are at all."

A home truth I'd already come to understand. At least two steps above annoyed, I hissed at her to remember the rules, did the two fingers pointing gesture from my eyes to hers to let her know I was watching her, and opened the door.

"What is going on in here?" Patrea surged through the door.

"Nothing," I said, and then thought better of the lie. "Actually, it's not nothing. I just found out that Paul did an interview and basically threw me under the bus."

"And?" She said as though I'd left out some important detail.

"And what? Isn't that enough? He lied about me knowing it would be on the TV news," I growled through my teeth.

37

"The man boinked another woman in your own bed and forged your name on legal documents, why on earth wouldn't he stoop to lying about you?"

"He did what, now?" Amber stomped all over one of the cardinal rules. You can't burn a ghost with a look, I know, because I tried.

Because Patrea hadn't heard Amber, she kept on talking. "Tell me what you've learned."

"Just that he said I was the one who misappropriated restricted funding and he ended the marriage when he found out what I'd done. What I'd done...doesn't that just fry my bacon."

I was almost mad enough to tell Patrea to go ahead and do her worst to him. Almost. My refusal to turn her loose had more to do with my conscience than the tender feelings she thought I still harbored for Paul. Those were now as dead as Amber.

"Tell her he says he has proof, and that he played the injured party to the hilt." I relayed Amber's message.

"Are you sure? Who told you all of this? Do you still have friends in the family?"

"Yes, I'm sure. It doesn't matter how I found out, the information is good, and no, I don't have friends in the family, but he says he has proof it was me. He can't possibly."

Patrea was excited now. "I don't even care how it happened because this is gold for our case. Can you find out more?"

"No, I—How is this gold?"

"If I can figure out how to change locations, I could go dig up some dirt." Amber made the offer, and I wondered what was in it for her. Well, other than my help in escaping the plane between this world and the next, which she didn't seem especially eager to do.

"The best defense is a good offense and knowing the other side's strategy will help us formulate our plan of attack. Can you get more?"

"—Maybe. I'll have to let you know."

With the revelation over, half of Patrea's attention turned toward the desk where I was seated. "Do you have anyone over there who'll take your side if...no, when the feds show up?" she said as she stroked a hand over fine-grained oak, and nudged me out of the way to check the fit of the drawers and drop-down top.

"The desk is not for sale."

"I'm just looking. It's a fine piece. Really. Mint condition." Her focus switched back from admiring an antique to the matter of proving my innocence. "Do you?"

"Do I what?" It took me a moment to catch up. "Oh! Albert might. He collected my personal items from my office when they let me go, and he always had a kind word for me when I came to work."

Still poking around in my desk, Patrea asked, "This Albert, what position does he hold in the organization? Does he have any authority?"

"Only when it comes to letting people in the building."

Having stayed quiet up until now, Amber burst out. "The doorman? They let the doorman go into your office? Doesn't that seem odd to you?"

"He's security." I elaborated more for Amber's benefit than Patrea's.

After a moment's consideration, Patrea asked, "Is he your mole?"

"Did she just call me a rodent?" The room temperature dropped a couple of degrees when Amber's temper got riled up. "I'm a journalist, not some common snitch."

The best I could do was give Amber a look behind Patrea's back. Juggling conversations between the living and the dead took more finesse than I was feeling at the moment.

"I haven't seen or spoken to Albert since the day he gently ushered me out of the building. He was as sweet as he could be under the circumstances. A true gentleman. He even carried my things to the car."

39

When she clapped her hands in delight, I tossed Patrea a raised eyebrow. "You seem pretty excited. I'm not sure why, though."

"Oh honey, you have no idea what a boon this is. You might have been the head of fundraising, but trust me, cleaning staff and security always have the best dirt. If this Albert person can be swayed to your side, we'll have a fountain of inside information."

Somehow I doubted the stalwart Albert would turn traitor, but I agreed to consider reaching out to him if Patrea deemed it necessary.

"Okay, that's settled. Now, if you don't mind, I'd like to go to bed." The lie tripped off my tongue. I doubted if Amber planned to let me sleep.

If the look in her eyes was anything to go by, Patrea would probably scheme the night away whether I sent her to her room or not, but juggling two conversations at once was off the table. Once she'd gone, I ordered Amber away so I could take a moment to process this new twist.

My mother had warned me Paul was bad news long before I'd married him. I'd been so angry with her I'd deliberately let our relationship turn cool, but she'd been right all along. That was just one point against him, though to be fair, it was more a point against me. There had been others that I had ignored until it was too late.

In hindsight, the flaws in our marriage became glaringly obvious. I'd let him isolate me from most of the people in my past without realizing his actions had been deliberate. Had he been sleeping with Reva all along?

Probably. And now that the blinders were off, I could see how he pushed me to become close friends with her. Since the moment I'd walked in and saw her face beneath his in a moment of passion, I'd done everything I could to bar thoughts of her from my head.

A double betrayal for which I'd blamed him more than her. I'd assumed Reva had fallen victim to Paul's magnetism because when he wanted to, he could pour on the charm like syrup over pancakes. Stupidly, when he'd used his wiles on me, a virtual nobody, I'd assumed it was true love. I had nothing to offer him other than myself, and so I'd signed the prenuptial agreement, quit school, and married him with the expectation of happily ever after.

Like most people, Patrea couldn't understand my reluctance to go after what she thought should rightly be mine—payment for his betrayal. Or maybe for the time I'd spent with him when I could have been with someone who genuinely loved me.

Putting a monetary value on my affections would make them feel as cheap as Paul seemed to think they were. Maybe, as Patrea insisted, I was putting pride before common sense, but when I'd walked away, my pride was the only thing Paul hadn't been able to lay claim to or tarnish.

Working for the charity, I learned how money, when used as a tool for good, can change a life. And how, when used as tool for control, how it can corrupt and corrode a person.

Paul could keep his money, with my blessing. I didn't need it, and moreover, I didn't want a single penny of it whether Patrea liked it or not.

# CHAPTER 7

My doorbell began ringing at six the next morning and didn't stop as a steady stream of Amber's co-workers and competition angled for my take on her death.

"No comment," Patrea whipped open the door, shouted at the top of her lungs, then slammed the door hard enough to shake the house. "Which one of those words is too difficult for these jokers to comprehend?" For some odd reason, seeing her rattled calmed me.

After a long night of introspection, I was too tired to hold back a smile. "You know, I thought you were the original ice queen before I got to know you better. Patrea Heard, the unflappable attorney with nerves of steel and a titanium spine."

"I'm taking that as a compliment, though I can't quite tell if you meant it that way."

Grinning at Patrea openly now, I handed her the cup of coffee she'd left behind on her way to the door. "You're not as intimidating to me as you seemed before, but then again, I've seen you in your jammies. I'd still hate to get on your bad side, though."

The doorbell chimed again.

"If it wasn't an antique, I'd take a hammer to that thing just to put an end to the noise."

I tapped the heel of my palm against my forehead. "Now that you mention it, there's a way to adjust the tone. David showed it to me when I moved in, but I didn't pay that much attention since I didn't expect to have a lot of company."

So saying, I went to the kitchen for a chair to stand on, and felt around the chime for the little lever that would reposition the hammer farther from the bell.

We didn't have long to wait to hear the results. My feet barely hit the floor before the chime gave off a muted tink-tonk that was far less annoying than the resounding bing-bong we'd been hearing all morning.

"Bless you, David," Patrea said, "Wherever you are." Taking her coffee, she headed toward the living room. "The local news will be on in a few minutes. Should be interesting."

I couldn't disagree when I saw Amber pacing the living room. "It's about time you got in here. Hurry up and turn on the TV so I can see what they're saying about me."

She ignored the glare I sent her way, and settled into the chair where I normally sat.

Touching ghosts is not my idea of fun. Talk about unpleasant sensations. Imagine putting your hand into iced, slimy water and then walking into a cobweb occupied by a half-dollar sized spider with hairy legs that then drops down the back of your neck.

Once you have that sensation firmly entrenched in your mind, double it and add a dose of the *monster under the bed* fear you had as a child.

It didn't matter that none of the ghosts I'd encountered so far had been malicious, their touch still gave me the creeps, so I sat on the sofa next to Patrea and flipped on channel five.

The camera moved in close to show morning anchor Ken Allen's features carefully arranged into a study of solemn lines. "It is with great sadness we announce the loss of one of our own."

A photo of Amber flashed on the screen. Probably the head-shot from her resume since it looked like a professional portrait. Her face turned slightly to the left, Amber presented a half-smile beneath a direct gaze with one eyebrow raised just enough to flirt but not so much that she came off as insincere.

The color of her blouse matched her eyes, and she wore a simple gold locket around her neck.

"Great sadness, my ass." Amber burst out. "The only thing that Tom Brokaw wannabe is sad about is that he can't accidentally brush his hand over my boob under the guise of adjusting my ear-piece anymore. The man's a lecherous jerk, which is why he'd been asked to leave. The official line is that he's moving on to a better job, but the truth is he's out and since I scored that interview with your ex, everyone knew the job was mine."

I wanted to ask for more details, but I couldn't say anything with Patrea right there, so I did my best to tune out Amber's diatribe. A feat which became far more difficult when the camera panned out to show another young woman sitting next to Ken, implying she'd be the one taking his place instead.

The banner under the new girl's name read 'Mia James', and she looked like a fish out of water. At least twice, she stumbled over her lines, and Amber snorted with each mistake.

Of course, my name came up in connection with finding the body while Patrea's wasn't mentioned. "That's not fair. He made it sound like I was skulking around some dark alley by myself when I came upon the body of poor, murdered Amber. Why didn't he mention you were there?"

"Hey, that didn't sound very flattering," Amber said, and I ignored that comment, too.

"You're front page news right now, and I'm not."

Sure enough, the mention of my name turned into a segue for more speculation about Paul and his family. Amber wasn't mentioned again until close to the wrap-up, and then only with a pithy statement about her loss.

"It could have been worse. They didn't play Paul's interview."

"Wait for it," Amber said darkly.

"It's not over yet," Patrea glowered at the television.

"Join us at five for an exclusive interview with Paul Hastings," Mia's smarmy voice continued. "It's one you won't want to miss."

Amber hooted. "Prime time. Station's counting on a ratings boost."

"Wonderful. We'll have that to look forward to after a day being stuck inside while the press batters at the door. What do you say, Patrea? More holiday romance or should we play Parcheesi while we wait? I feel like a rat in a cage."

"Hell, no. What were your plans for the day before all this came up?"

"Decorating Christmas cookies with my folks. It's one of our traditions, but I don't want to drag them into the line of fire if I can help it." Not that my mother couldn't hold her own. She could tear a strip off you without breaking a sweat if you did something to incur her wrath. "I'm sure that sounds boring to you, but it would have been fun."

A misty smile spread over Patrea's face. "I think it sounds like an experience I wouldn't want to miss. We'll go."

"What about the reporters? Won't they follow us?"

Instead of answering, Patrea asked me another question. "Do you trust me?"

Before I answered, I assessed her mood and it bordered on playful. The kind of playful a cat exhibits just before pouncing on an unsuspecting mouse. Whatever she was planning, I wasn't sure it boded well for the reporters on my front steps.

"I trust you," but I had to be honest, "even if I'm a hundred percent positive you're going to ask me to do something I won't like."

"It's time," Patrea said, "to give the press a statement."

That wasn't so bad, and it should get them off my back. The last thing I wanted was to become Debbie Downer spending Christmas holed up in the house with the curtains drawn.

"Everly, you need to put your side of the story out before they air that interview, and you need to play the cheating card like it was your ace in the hole. You need to be on the noon edition of the news and you need to name names."

Stunned, I felt the blood drain out of my face, then shoot back up to flame and burn my cheeks.

"She's right." Amber piped up. I'd almost forgotten about her because she'd gone quiet. "If you do an interview first, they'll air some or all of it along with his. It's the only way to get ahead of this. Paul already has a leg up on you because of his family connections. If you don't name and shame, he's going to control the arc, and you'll come off looking exactly how he planned."

"Okay. I don't like it, but I think you're right. He was counting on me to value privacy above scandal. But he asked for whatever he gets, and I can't see any other way to handle the situation."

Patrea let out a sigh of relief. "I figured I'd have to fight you tooth and nail, but for once, you took the sensible route. There's one more thing."

She didn't need to say it, I already knew. "It all has to come out, even the stuff about the prenup." I sighed, and covered my face with my hands.

"You didn't do anything wrong." Patrea leaned over and gently tugged my hand back down, then moved until her face was directly in my line of vision. "You're the victim here, and there's no shame in that. So what if you fell for the wrong man? It happens every day, but he did more than just cheat, so now you have to make a choice to become a survivor and that means being proactive. Right now. Today."

I nodded miserably.

"Don't envy me my titanium spine. Those are easy to come by. You just have to stand up, and you won't be standing alone."

Grammie Dupree always said if you cut off your nose to spite your face, you won't be able to smell the roses. I know she was mixing metaphors, but she said if you're going to do a thing, don't half-ass it. Her wisdom might be homey, and most of the time a little bawdy, but my grandmother lived her life on her terms right up until the end. She wouldn't be proud of me for doing less.

"Let's get dressed. I want to look my best if I'm going to be on camera."

Amber let out a whoop that made me jump, and the jumping made Patrea look at me quizzically. I shrugged it off, and headed to my room to change while she announced to the reporters that I would make a statement as long as it aired by noon.

While I put on my makeup, Amber gave me the inside scoop on Paul's interview and coached me on the best way to refute his pack of lies.

"You've gotta hand it to him for having a smooth tongue." Taking a few deep breaths, I pushed back both fury and nerves to keep from poking myself in the eye with a mascara wand. "I suppose you bought that crap hook, line, and sinker."

"Excuse me, how was I supposed to know any different? I did come here and try to give you a chance to tell your side of things. At least give me credit for that much. Plus, I'm on your side now. I can be a real asset to the team."

"Until I figure out who killed you, and then you'll go into the light where you belong."

Amber pursed her lips. "Naturally. But you don't need to rush on that, do you?"

She'd be the first ghost not to bug me endlessly on that score. "You want to hang around?"

"There are worse things I could be doing, and besides, I feel partly responsible for putting you in a tight spot."

Dressed in high, 1940s style, Patrea poked her head in, "It's time."

I hoped she hadn't heard me talking to Amber, but if she did, her face revealed nothing.

"Are you sure we should do this on the front porch? Wouldn't it be better to ask them inside?"

"We'll use every tactic at our disposal including psychological warfare. You standing two steps above them sends a subtle message."

When butterflies threatened to turn my stomach into an air show, I took a deep breath and put on my game face. The one I'd used during events to talk the wealthy out of funding for the poor. It wasn't my fault some of that funding went into Paul's family's pockets, and no matter what he said, I refused to take the blame.

The scruffy-looking guy who had wielded the camera for Amber stood next to a field reporter in a suit and represented channel five. Both of the other local network affiliates had sent their own crews, and I was glad it was winter and not the early weeks of spring, otherwise they'd have created a mud puddle out of my front yard. Although, upon further reflection, watching them all have to wade through a foot of mud would have been quite entertaining.

"Lance, make sure you get my good side," the reporter said, his tone brusque and demeaning. Say what you want about Amber, but I doubted she talked to her crew like that.

"Sure thing, Gary."

"Mrs. Hastings, did you know your husband was embezzling funds from his family's charity?" The perky redhead from channel two asked such an uninspired question it made me want to stick my tongue out at her.

"It's Miss Dupree now, and no, I had no dealings with the corporate side of my husband's business."

"And how is that possible?" the reporter shot back, her eyes steely now.

I resisted the urge to reach out and slap the smug look off her face even as Amber said, "Don't do it," and instead regurgitated the answer Patrea had drilled into my head.

"The philanthropic arm and the corporate arm of my husband's family business operated out of different locations, he worked at one while I worked at the other. I didn't answer directly to him, nor he to me. Paul rarely spoke about his work, and now that his indiscretions have come to light, I understand why."

The questions came in rapid fire after that. With a bit of coaching from Amber and keeping it simple, I gave my statement, answering everything thrown at me with the truth. Amber's replacement, Gary, who was far less pushy than she'd been, had barely managed to direct two queries in my direction before another car marked with the channel five number pulled into the driveway, skidding to a stop and flinging snow everywhere.

"Oh, there you are, Lance. There's been a change of plan." Mia James, I recognized her from the morning report, shoved her way through the knot of reporters without offering so much as a hint of apology for interrupting. "I'm in, he's out." She pointed a thumb toward Gary who clenched his fists and set his jaw, but didn't bother to argue with her. Probably, I assumed, because she was above him on the hierarchy or because she wouldn't have listened anyway.

Mia proceeded to delay the interview for a few more seconds while she pulled out a compact, dabbed some powder on her nose, used the mirror to check her lipstick, and adjusted the collar of the button-up shirt where it stuck out from beneath her sweater.

I barely registered when Amber blinked out to wherever it is she went when she wasn't harassing me, but by that time I was in a groove and didn't need her coaching anyway.

"Miss Dupree," Mia shouted an octave higher than the rest of the horde, grabbing my attention. "Why did you divorce Mr. Hastings then, if you had no idea about the misappropriated funds?"

I considered her question, and it infuriated me to think that I shouldn't be expected to have another reason besides criminal activity for which to be unhappy in my marriage. The weight of undeserved shame fell off of me as I spoke convincingly of coming home to find my husband in bed with a woman I'd considered my friend and confidant. The crowning moment, at least for me, came when I looked right at the camera and warned other women that emotional abuse comes in many forms, and a controlling husband was an abusive one.

No, Paul had never hit me, but he'd left plenty of bruises on my psyche. Bruises that were still healing. I bared my soul, maybe more than I'd planned. When it came time to talk about the forgery, I handed the baton to Patrea. If I'd known how cathartic telling my story would be, I might have done it the first time Patrea suggested I should.

When the door closed behind the reporters, I sank onto the sofa and let the tears come while Patrea put an awkward arm around my shoulders. The spate only lasted a minute or two, but when it was over, I felt washed clean and baptized by fire.

"Was that what you wanted?" I asked her. "Did I hit all the talking points?"

"Honey, you were a force," Patrea said, "you almost made me cry, and that's no mean feat."

"He's going to come off looking like the world's biggest asshole," Amber didn't censor herself. "Which is exactly what he is. A rotten egg wrapped up in a charming package still smells bad, and boy does he stink."

Thanks to Amber's inside knowledge, I thought I avoided saying anything that could be too badly misconstrued, and I felt lighter than I had in months.

"I hate to say it, but you were right. I should have done this ages ago, but I felt like such an idiot for being duped by a handsome man who knew all the right buttons to push."

Settling back, Patrea slipped of her shoes and propped her stockinged feet up on the coffee table. "We've all been there." She reached over to pat me on the knee.

"Okay," I used Amber's phrase on Patrea, "tit for tat. It's time you told me your sad story. I'm not taking no for an answer, and I want to know what you have against Paul while you're at it."

"I'm sure my story is far less scintillating than the one you've cooked up in that pretty head of yours."

"See, I heard you say pretty which sounds like a compliment, but it's not." I didn't care a whit about the dryness of her tone, that was Patrea's baseline and I'd come to learn she used sarcasm as a defense mechanism to keep people at a distance. Well, that wouldn't work with me.

With a wry twist of her head, Patrea continued. "I guess I should preface this by saying I'm sorry I didn't pull you aside the first day we met and tell you to run for the hills. But I didn't know you then, and by the time I realized you were exactly what you seemed it was too late."

"Apology accepted." I waved my hand to indicate she should get on with her story.

Sighing, she did. "I grew up with Paul Hastings. We went to the same school, lived in the same neighborhood, went to the same country club, the same parties."

"Were the two of you ever involved?"

"No." Patrea barked out a short laugh. "Not hardly. I'm a year older, and he went for the pretty but brainless. I've never been either of those things."

My face must have registered the emotional kick in the gut because she immediately countered the statement.

"There, I've gone and stuck my foot in my mouth again. I was never good at being a socialite. Too much bulldog in my nature is what makes me good at defending people, even if I'm horrible at befriending them. I don't think you're brainless. What I meant was that I saw past Paul's charm to the rotten core underneath."

After the way he'd treated me, I couldn't argue for him.

"What I meant was that he had a pattern when it came to girlfriends, and I didn't fit the mold. He screwed up with you, and I suspect once he realized his mistake, he spent some time trying to turn you into a suitable doormat."

51

"He did," I admitted. "I didn't see it at the time because it all happened so gradually, I didn't notice I was being cut off from my family and friends. Worse, he tried to poison me against them."

Patrea nodded. "Isolate and assimilate. Standard tactics for indoctrinating a disciple."

"You make it sound like I joined a cult or something." I was beginning to regret starting this conversation.

"Didn't you?" she countered. "Not willingly, but in theory, that's exactly what happened."

"So I really was brainless."

Eyes firing with fury, Patrea turned toward me. "Shut up. You know I didn't mean to imply that. Paul Hastings is a predator preying on the spineless. He screwed up when he picked you, and when he realized he couldn't keep you firmly under his thumb, he staged a scene."

My mouth dropped open as it all flooded back. Walking through my bedroom door to find my husband and my friend canoodling without a care in the world. Paul hadn't even tried to defend himself; he'd let his attorney drop the bomb on my life.

"Are you saying you think his timing was deliberate— that he not only let me catch him cheating, but meant for me to walk in when I did?"

Amber still hovered in my favorite chair taking in the conversation with avid interest, occasionally letting out a snort, but not saying anything. But Patrea countered my question with another.

"Don't you?"

I considered, and realized the theory made horrible sense.

"Well, now I do, but weren't we talking about you?" I needed a moment to process. "It seems like we're back on my problems again."

"I'm trying to establish a pattern."

"Once a cheater, always a cheater. Don't worry, I'm seeing the pieces fall into place without needing to hear about all of the women who went before me."

Settling back with a mirthless smile on her face, Patrea said, "I wasn't planning on trotting out a list of names. It goes much deeper than just his inability to stick to one woman at a time. My brother got kicked out of school because Paul cheated on a term paper, and then passed the blame off on Justin."

She went on to tell me how powerless she'd felt to help her brother, and how deeply he'd been scarred by the experience. Tears gathered, but Patrea held them back.

"My father spoke to the dean, tried to appeal the decision. Everyone knew what Paul had done. He bragged about it, so I'm certain the dean knew Justin was innocent, but Thurston Hastings wrote a check with a lot of zeros at the end, and the expulsion held. Even if he'd known what would happen, I'm not sure if my father would have resorted to buying back my brother's good name."

Since Patrea hadn't factored her brother in when she told me her Christmas plans, I assumed the worst. "What happened to Justin?"

"That's the hardest part. I'm not sure we'll ever know. The day after Thanksgiving, we found his room empty. Some of his things were missing so we know he packed a bag, but he disappeared without a trace. My father paid a fortune to private investigators over the years and not one of them ever turned up a clue."

"That's worse than the alternative," Amber said. "Always having to wonder is the hardest."

Her wistful tone sounded like she might have some experience to back up the statement, but I couldn't ask her about it with Patrea sitting between us.

Taking Patrea's hand, and squeezing with gentle pressure, I said, "I'm sorry."

No wonder she wanted to take my husband down.

53

# CHAPTER 8

After hearing Patrea's story, I offered to skip the Christmas cookie festivities if she wasn't feeling up to it, but she'd waved off the notion with an impatient hand.

"I try not to dwell on the past. You promised me the full small-town Christmas experience, and you're going to deliver. Now, are you sure I should wear this red checkered flannel and not the blue?"

Grinning, because she seemed to need a lighter mood, I teased, "The red is more festive, but I still think you should have sprung for that dirndl dress from Curiosities."

"Hey, I said cookie decorating reminded me of the 1950s, not that I wanted to dress the part. You've got me wearing jeans, isn't that bad enough?"

"Don't be such a clothes snob," I clipped on Molly's leash for the walk to the car. "Relax a little, and count your lucky stars. My dad wanted to make this an ugly sweater event, but my mom put her foot down."

Patrea shuddered. "You're sure they don't mind me tagging along?"

"Why would they? It's an open house type of party. Lots of people drop by to decorate a cookie or two. You'll see, it'll be fun."

Decked out in lights along the eaves and candles in every window, the house looked cheerful and warm when we pulled into the drive. Molly perked up as soon as she heard old Blue's welcoming bark, and practically dragged me up the steps.

"Craftsman. Excellent example of the style," Patrea observed with her usual appreciation for period architecture. "Lovely. Is the interior as well-preserved as the exterior?"

"Come on, you'll just have to see for yourself."

My hand closed over the knob just as the door opened, and my father pulled me in for one of his famous hugs. Everyone has a knack for something and putting people at ease was my father's. Or one of them, at any rate. He could also make a piece of wood practically beg to be turned into something beautiful.

When he let me go, I introduced Patrea and held back a grin at the panicked look on her face when she thought she was in for the same treatment. Dad read her face, too, and went with a solid, double handshake, then leaned down to give Molly's ears a good rub.

My father and my dog were their own mutual admiration society.

"Your mother's in the kitchen getting things ready. I'll let you put your coats away, and then you can join us there." To Molly he said, "Let's go find Blue." Prying the leash from my hand, he took my dog off toward the screened porch out back.

The heady scents of cinnamon, sugar, and chocolate filled the house.

"I'm gaining weight from the smell alone," Patrea groaned. "I can feel my thighs expanding by the minute."

"You're the size of a stick. I think you'll weather the storm." I took her coat and headed for the closet while she checked out the built-in shelving that my father had restored and my mother kept polished to a warm gleam.

"Whoever did the work on these shelves is a master. Most people would never know they'd been repaired. It takes a fine hand to match old patina so perfectly."

"I'll be sure to pass along your compliments to my dad. Unless you want to tell him yourself. Just be warned, he'll talk your ear off about the colors of stain and the merits of Tung oil."

Reverently, Patrea looked toward the kitchen. "You promise?"

Laughing, I said yes, and she followed me toward the sound of clanging pans.

The counters groaned under platters of cold meats, veggies with dip, bread, fruit, and cheese for snacking while we worked. I introduced Patrea again, hugged my mother, and nipped a shred of turkey off the platter.

"Did David make it to Vermont before the storm hit?" David was the son of an old friend of my father's, and for reasons of his own had been staying with my folks for a few months.

"Safe and sound." Mom slapped my fingers away from a grape tomato. "Get a plate first."

"Dan and Wendy Barrington have invited us to drive out and stay for New Year's," my father said. "Since it falls on a weekend, we thought we'd go if you don't mind having old Blue for a few days."

"I'd be happy to, and Molly would be thrilled to have a partner in crime."

A look passed between my parents. "What's wrong?"

"I don't think we should leave town with a killer on the loose. The way you attract trouble, I'd worry about you the whole time."

Sure, I get attacked by two crazed murderers and my mother thinks it's a trend.

"You should go. I didn't even know Amber Hale, there's no way her death is connected to me." Other than that she'd been in town because of me, but that was a coincidence, right? It had to be.

Winking at me, Dad said, "Enough talk about death in front of the cookies. You'll curdle the milk."

"Milk? There's eggnog, right? The good stuff, not that junk from the grocery store."

"Of course." Reaching out, my dad tugged on a lock of my hair just as the doorbell rang. "That'll be Jacy and Brian. I'll go let them in."

Despite Patrea's mock scorn, the tradition of cookie decorating in our house was a newer one. One that my father blamed on my mother's addiction to all things Martha Stewart and an episode featuring delicate blue and white snowflake cookies.

Needless to say, our first batch had not measured up to Martha's perfection, but we'd had so much fun we'd tried again the next night, and then the next. Now it wouldn't be Christmas without crumbs, friends, and sticky royal icing.

Plates of cookies covered the table, each one with a towel draped over the top. "That's more cookies than normal. How many people are coming?" Over the years, cookie decorating night had grown into an open house party.

"Oh, I'm not sure. The usual number, I suppose. You can blame your father for the...ahem...surfeit of sweets. He decided to try his hand at crafting cutters out of sheet metal this year, and you know him."

"Dad has a tendency to go overboard on a new project." I informed Patrea. "What could he possibly make that we didn't already have?" My mother's cookie cutter collection could rival her idol's with everything from angels to candy canes to wreaths.

"Don't laugh." She whipped the towel off one of the platters, and beside me, Patrea let out a husky laugh.

"Ugly sweater cookies."

"They seemed like a reasonable compromise," Mom said. "I'd rather eat them than wear them."

Returning with Brian and Jacy in tow, Dad caught the tail end of the conversation.

"I predict they'll be a hit," I said as the doorbell rang again. "I'll get it."

"That'll be Neena." Jacy came with. "She wasn't going to come, but I threatened her with grievous bodily injury if she didn't."

"Everything okay?"

"Viola," Jacy only had time to grind the word out from between her teeth before we got to the door. On the other side, Neena's face was white with splotches of high color along her cheeks. Once she handed her guitar case to Jacy, I gave her a hug because it looked like she needed one, and took her coat.

"Don't ask. I don't want to talk about it now. If my blood pressure goes any higher, my head'll explode."

"Again? I thought you made up." I sympathized. Viola Montayne had been, and technically I supposed, was still Neena's mother-in-law. Having dated Hudson Montayne during high school, I had experienced firsthand, how Viola had doted upon her son. As far as she was concerned, he'd hung the moon and the stars, and no woman would ever be good enough for her baby. When he'd been murdered in June, Viola—as expected—hadn't taken the news with any sort of aplomb. She'd turned on poor Neena faster than a striking snake.

"We did, but now I'm wondering if I wasn't better off when she hated me. She...never mind, I have no words, and I smell cookies." Turning, Neena took the guitar case from Jacy and stood it up in a corner out of the way. "Why don't you load me up with holiday cheer, and we'll leave off talking about the spawn of Satan. I'm afraid if we keep saying her name, we'll conjure her up out of thin air."

But mention of Viola had reminded me, "What with everything else that happened last night, I never did find out who won the lighting contest."

"Oh, now that's a story I don't mind tellin'," Neena perked up. "This is all hearsay, because with everything else, I didn't dare to ask her, but according to the rumor mill a group of concerned citizens staged a protest. Viola was knocked out of the runnin' because she hired out to a professional, so Doug and Charlene Partridge took first place."

"Hey," Brian poked his head out of the kitchen, "less chattering, more partying. Get in here so we can eat."

While I fixed a plate, I caught the time out of the corner of my eye. If Amber had been right in her prediction, my ex-husband's lying face would be splashed all over the news by now, but I refused to let him mar the day.

"I've missed this, you know." I said when I got a chance to talk to my mother alone. "I didn't realize how much I let Paul pull me away from home and family until I came back."

Never again, I vowed to myself. Never again would I let a man have sway over me. Never again would a man stand between me and my family. Never again.

As the evening wore on, Neena broke out her guitar for a Christmas carol sing-a-long, and Patrea shocked us all with Oh, Holy Night in a perfect contralto that put tears in my mother's eyes.

People came and went, but not as many as in past years. Noting the absences, I asked my mother, "Where are all the canasta ladies? They never miss cookie night."

"Sick with the flu."

Overhearing, Patrea grimaced, "You mean the plague. Half the time I had it, I was afraid I was going to die, the other half, I wished I would and get it over with. If Everly hadn't given me whatever witch's brew she got from…. Leandra, I think it was…I'd still be coughing up my lungs."

Jacy toasted the comment with virgin eggnog. "Behold the properties of the elderberry. Next best thing to magic." Turning to my mom, she said, "My mom has enough syrup stored up in the pantry to treat the whole town for the next two years. I'd be happy to drop a few bottles off at the library tomorrow if you'd like. Then you can distribute it to those who need it most."

"That would be lovely, dear. Since we're on the subject," Mom fixed me with a look that I'd seen many times before.

"Barbara Dexter could use a hand out at the Bide-A-Way tomorrow, and I've already told her you'd be happy to clean a couple of rooms."

It wasn't the first time my mother had volunteered me for something, but when I'd returned to town Mrs. Dexter had given me a deal on a room at the motel, and then we'd found a body together. That kind of thing forms a bond. Plus, the work might allow me a chance to sneak into Amber's room and see if there were any clues to her murder just lying around.

"I'll help, too." Patrea offered, and when I caught the subtle waggle of her left eyebrow, I assumed she'd had a similar thought.

Ignoring the frisson of guilt over having an ulterior motive, I basked for a moment in the warmth of my mother's smile. "I'll drop off some of Leandra's cure while I'm there.

"What was in that eggnog?" Patrea wobbled a little getting into the car once the party ran down.

"It's dad's special recipe. I'm not sure what he puts in it, but it packs a punch if you have more than one glass of the special, spiked version."

"Oh," Patrea grinned, "That explains why I feel so good right now. Your parents are aces, did you know that? They made me feel right at home, and I think I've talked your dad into building me some shelves."

The compliment gave me a glow that had nothing to do with the half glass of special eggnog I'd consumed during the evening. "I'm glad you stayed."

# CHAPTER 9

"Shall we?" Back at my place, Patrea pointed the remote and pulled up the DVR menu as Molly draped her warm body over my feet.

Sighing, I nodded and prepared to let my giddy holiday happiness fade away. I'd eaten too many cookies and now they sat in my stomach like rocks.

"It's better if we know what we're up against." A shower and changing into her pajamas seemed to have mellowed Patrea's eggnog buzz.

Maybe for her, but I'd rather eat my arm than spend a minute staring at Paul's face. As luck would have it, I didn't have to.

"That's weird. I must have missed it." Patrea hit stop, restarted the broadcast, and fast-forwarded more slowly.

Relief swept over me. "Or they decided not to air his interview after all."

"His father probably threw wads of money at someone to make it go away. Unless Paul's handling that type of thing himself these days. Our little boy is all grown up."

Molly grumbled when I pulled my feet out from under her and sprawled them over the arm of the chair. "Paul is a last word kind of guy. I can't imagine him making the effort to have the interview pulled. He'd want to get his story out there, and he'd expect to be believed. It wouldn't occur to him that anyone might doubt his word. Attitude of the rampantly spoiled, I think."

"They didn't pull the interview. The recording went missing." My left eye twitched when Amber popped in without warning. "Oh, and by the way, I've figured out how to go places. Sort of. I could really get to like this ghost gig. You want me to spy on your ex? I've got you covered."

Great, I thought, more information I had to hold back from Patrea because I couldn't reveal my source.

Or could I? What would the analytically inclined lawyer think if I told her there was a ghost sitting two feet to her right? Could she feel the chill in the air that always came with close proximity to the not-quite-departed? She'd asked if the house was haunted, and not in a mocking way.

The real question was did I have the guts to try? After some consideration, the answer was no, so I directed a subtle head shake at Amber, and made Patrea an offer.

"It shouldn't take long to clean up a couple of motel rooms in the morning, why don't we go over to your place after so you can pick up some extra clothes? And, unless they've changed his hours, I know what time Albert clocks off work on Wednesdays. We can wait for him in the parking lot and see what he has to say."

Pursing her lips, Patrea weighed the suggestion. "Okay, but you never mentioned maid work as part of your hometown Christmas experience. This isn't turning out like the movies at all."

"Sure it is," I said. "This is the part where you learn that serving others selflessly brings out the spirit of giving. You'll clean, and you'll feel uplifted by the spirit of Christmas."

"You're only saying that so you won't have to do it alone. Fine, I'll concede the point, but where's the hunky man with the complicated past who vows never to love again until we meet, when I practically fall at his feet because my heels are too high?"

"You never said you were trolling for a holiday romance. I'll have to see what I can do about that." Not that I had a clue what type of man she might like, or who in town was free.

Men of the dating persuasion hadn't been on my radar since I'd moved back, so I hadn't been paying attention. Nor did I plan to for myself, but if Patrea wanted a fling, Jacy would know who was on the market.

"Unless you've got a magic wand up your…sleeve, I'd say your chances of pulling that off are somewhere around the size of a gnat's ass. I'm not the type men fall for at first sight."

Tilting my head, I assessed Patrea as objectively as I could. Because I'd seen her in action, I knew a heart of gold beat under a gruff exterior that she put on to hide any sign of weakness. Patrea needed a strong man because she'd roll right over a weaker one and he'd never stand a chance.

Physically, I could admit it would be a stretch to ever call Patrea beautiful just based on her looks, but she wasn't a plain-looking woman, either. What was most attractive about her came from a vitality that lit her up from the inside out. Any man who couldn't see that didn't deserve her anyway.

"Then you've been meeting the wrong men. You're a catch."

She snorted, "Catch and release is more like it."

Sticking with the fishing metaphor, I said, "Maybe because you keep fighting the line so hard. When was the last time you went out on a date?"

"Do you want the month or the year? Because I know it's been a couple since the last time I scared a man off. It's surprisingly easy to do, you know. All it takes is a little honesty, and they're out the door before dessert."

Intrigued, I asked for an example.

"Well, there was this one man who took me to a nice restaurant, and then said something to the effect that eating there was probably a treat for me. I can't even take credit for what happened with that one because the waiter came over and greeted me by name. Then the owner, a personal friend of mine, sent out appetizers, and my date acted like I'd asked *him* there to show off instead of the other way around."

63

Patrea held out the box of ribbon candy, and I chose a pink piece, letting the cinnamon sweetness warm my mouth before asking if he'd called again.

"No. He took his injured pride along with the piece of cheesecake the chef boxed up for me, and left me to call a cab."

"I think that's the worst first/last date story I've ever heard."

But Patrea had more.

"That one? That one was nothing compared to the five-foot wonder who informed me the only reason he'd asked me out was because I was tall. He didn't take it very well when I replied that I'd only accepted because I'd thought he was intelligent, but I guessed only one of us got it right. That one didn't even make it to appetizers."

No wonder she'd lost confidence in men. And here I was, the last person in the world who should argue the counterpoint, lining up my thoughts on why Patrea should try dating again. Except she beat me to it.

"I've been on some bad dates, but who hasn't? I'm sure those men and others like them tell bad date stories about me, too. Men aren't so bad, it's the dating part that I really hate. All those expectations, and the posturing. What I'd really like is to cut through all that and just find someone who is genuine enough to feel the same way so we can move right past the awkward stuff."

I nodded as if I agreed, but didn't tell Patrea that my dating experience was pretty much limited to two men. One I'd met in high school, and one I'd married. In between I'd gone out on a double date or two, but nothing on the scale of what Patrea described.

"That's why I binge movies this time of year—to get my annual dose of love at first sight. Meet before Christmas, fight the feeling for a minute, then give in and accept the happily ever after before Santa's fat backside disappears back up the chimney."

"It sounds so romantic when you put it like that."

"However it sounds, I'm not the type of woman to rouse a man to flights of romantic fancy," she said matter-of-factly. "If I ever get married, it won't be to the hot guy with a hammer in his back pocket who shows up to fix the pipes at the country inn I magically inherit from some relative I haven't seen in fifteen years. It will be to that guy's accountant after he's worn me down by the logic of not wanting to end up alone."

Having recently taken up a job in the rental upkeep sector, I declined to point out that any handyman who used nothing but a hammer on pipes might be hunky, but probably wouldn't enjoy long-term employment in the industry.

"I'm just not cut out for romance. Especially not the holiday kind. My mother should have named me Holly or Merry, or Carol to at least give me a sporting chance. Even Chris would work." Good-natured humor threaded through her tone, and there was a smirk on her face. A facade? Maybe. With Patrea, it was hard to tell.

Lifting the remote, Patrea tapped the DVR button and scrolled through the options. "For now, let's live vicariously through—," she made her choice, "—Noelle, the ice sculptor who gets stranded in a small town during a blizzard. I feel something of kinship with her already."

# CHAPTER 10

In the morning, I found Patrea drinking coffee in the tower room and enjoying the way the rising sun teased pink glints from the thin layer of snow that had fallen during the night. Winking Christmas lights faded to colored sparkles in the brightening dawn.

"I'm a city girl, through and through, but I could get used to this view. It's too bad the space isn't big enough for a bed, or you might have trouble getting rid of me."

Cradling a hot cup in my hands, I moved closer to the windows. "It's a restful spot. Catherine Willowby used to come up here and take pictures. I found her camera on the table when I moved in." There'd been a stack of notebooks as well, but in all the excitement of settling in they'd ended up stashed somewhere, and I hadn't had a chance to look at them. "One of these days, I'll hunt down someone who still develops film and see if they're any good."

Taking her cue from the former occupant, Patrea went down the narrow flight of stairs and came back with her phone to snap a few shots. I even let her drag me in for an unexpected selfie using the town as a backdrop.

"I'm starving," Patrea said. "Feed me breakfast before you force me into menial labor. I think that's a fair trade."

"I could go for silver dollar pancakes and bacon, or maybe a loaded omelet. We'll hit the Blue Moon on the way, and since we're running early, save ourselves a stop at the library to pick up the elderberry flu-killer. Jacy's working this morning."

The few minutes we spent outside with Molly turned both our noses pink, and even the dog was feeling the cold. She cut her morning romp down to the bare minimum, then raced up to the door, dropped to her haunches, and gave me her hurry-up look. When I let her back inside, she shook the snow off her coat and made a beeline for her favorite sunny spot on the kitchen floor.

"Nope, we're taking my car," Patrea said when I headed toward the garage. "It's full of gas, has heated seats, and it's better on the snow."

"You had me at heated seats." Gratefully, I climbed inside and flipped the switch. In moments, warmth stole through my chilled flesh. "Turn left at the end of the street, and then right when you get to the main drag."

The drive to the diner was all too short, and I hated to leave the warm comfort for the penetrating cold, but the tantalizing scents of coffee and bacon wafted out into the parking lot, and I chose hunger over a warm behind.

"Is the food as good as it smells?"

"Better," Jacy answered for me as she stepped up to take our order. Then she leaned down and whispered, "Leo showed up early and finally made his move this morning. I'll take my break and tell you about it when your order's up."

"Who's Leo, and what's going on?" Patrea wanted to know once Jacy had gone.

"Leo's my boss, and he's had a thing for Mabel for just about forever, but he didn't know how to speak up, I guess, so he drank his coffee and pined in silence."

"Until this morning." Returning in time to hear the explanation, Jacy poured cups of coffee and left us with more than one appetite whetted. Curiosity turned the minutes long before she plunked down our plates and slid in beside me.

I took one look at my platter of pancakes and let out a snort. "I take it Mabel was pleased."

"What? How do you know?" Patrea was in the dark.

67

"Well, she's not normally prone to putting whipped cream smiley faces on the pancakes." Mabel and whimsy hadn't been acquainted.

"Oh, it went well, all right." Without asking, Jacy transferred half her omelet to my plate and snagged half my pancakes. "I knew something was up when he walked through the door. He'd gone and got himself a haircut, and I don't mean his usual chop job. I think he spent some money at an actual barbershop or salon."

As far as I knew, Jacy had no idea what Leo's net worth might be, but working for him, I'd discovered he was loaded—by Mooselick River standards, anyway.

"And that's not all. He had on a fancy new set of duds. It's the first time I've ever seen the man wearing clothes that didn't look older than me."

I'd had a talk with Leo a few months back about how he shouldn't underestimate himself, but it hadn't seemed to stick. Or maybe, like he did with everything else, Leo had taken the time to ruminate awhile.

"I think I'm getting the picture," Patrea cast a look toward the kitchen where Mabel worked. "This Leo, he's a little guy, right? Shy and well-meaning, but on the scrawny side compared to her."

Brawny was a good word to describe the diner owner, but only if you meant it in the nicest way. Nobody messed with Mabel, but everyone knew she'd feed you even if you didn't have money until payday.

I forked up a bite of pancake and swirled it through the leftover syrup on my plate. "Yep, you nailed it. Nice guy, not one to speak up much, though."

"Until today." Jacy grinned. "And when he let go, he went the distance." She spooned a bite of ketchup-dotted omelet into the middle of one of her miniature pancakes, dumped syrup over the top, folded up the pancake, and popped it into her mouth while Patrea stared in horror. "Sorry, it's the baby. The little peanut is a weird eater."

As if to dispel the visual, Patrea shook her head.

"Stop teasing," I said, "I want the details."

"You know that scene in Say Anything with the boombox and all?"

I paused with my coffee cup only a whisper away from my lips. "No. Leo pulled a Lloyd Dobbler? I can't even picture that." That was a lie. I could picture it, I just couldn't reconcile the image that formed in my head.

"Not exactly, but he did make a grand gesture." Pausing again, Jacy seemed to be struggling with how to relay what had happened, partly because she couldn't stop smiling. "Did you know Leo could sing?"

"Sing?" I repeated.

"Yeah, sing. Like he could be on stage somewhere."

I put my fork down. "You're kidding."

"I am not. I was in the back when he started in, and she just went stone still. Terry had to pull the spatula out of her hand and flip the sausage. At first, I couldn't see who was singing, because Mabel stepped in front of me and took half an age to go through the door."

"I have to ask," Patrea broke in at that point, "what was the song?"

"That's the most surreal part. I'd have put my whole salary down on the fact that Leo Hanson couldn't pick Mariah Carey out of a lineup, but there he was belting out All I Want for Christmas is You."

After our discussion the previous evening, I knew why Patrea turned and appraised Mabel dispassionately.

Still, I had to know. "What did she say?"

"Well, she just stood there and you couldn't tell what she was thinking, but that didn't stop Leo. He finished the song, popped his chin in the air, and said, 'I think it's time we went on a date.'" Eyes twinkling, Jacy finished the story. "She never even cracked a smile when she told him to pick her up at seven and if he was late, she'd sic the dog on him."

That part I had no trouble picturing.

"But when she turned around, her eyes were sparkling."

"I wish I'd been there to see it all in person, but good for Leo. It's about time."

With an even bigger grin, Jacy said, "If he'd waited one more day, I'd have missed it, too. Today's my last day."

Since opening Curated Collections with Neena, Jacy had been working two jobs, but between her burgeoning belly and swollen ankles, something had to give. "The shop is doing so well, I don't need two jobs, and Brian's been after me to quit waiting tables. Neena, too."

"Congratulations," I gave her a one-armed hug. "Why didn't you say anything the night of the lighting contest?"

"I wasn't sure I could go through with it. I've had this job so long it's hard to let it go, but Mabel was wonderful about everything. She's like a hazelnut, you know? Prickly on the outside, with a meaty, slightly sweet center."

The metaphor made me smile. "I'm not sure you should say that to her face, because it might come off a little weird." I pulled out my wallet. "I hate to eat and run, but we need to get out to the Bide-A-Way." While I paid for breakfast, Jacy fetched the bottle of elderberry syrup.

"Not a bad meal. The food was almost as tasty as the gossip," Patrea rated the diner as we pulled away. "This Leo, did he really pine for Mabel for years before making his move?"

"He did. See, didn't I tell you? Small town holiday romance is alive and well."

# CHAPTER 11

Other than to ask for directions, Patrea was quiet during the rest of the short drive.

Barbara Dexter looked like death warmed over when she handed me her master keys. "'Preciate the help," she said, and looked scornfully at the bottle of jewel-colored syrup I handed her. "You sure this won't kill me? What's in it?"

"Elderberries and whatever else Leandra Wade thinks is good for you, I guess. All I know is it works. Which rooms do you need cleaned?"

"I guess we'll see about that. Anyhow, the dead girl was in one. Ernie's done combing the place for clues, so he said. We have the fellow with the camera in four, and then there's seven." Mrs. Dexter put a hand to her head. "That one should be a piece of cake. A couple of elderly ladies got caught out in the storm on their way back from Hackinaw."

"Isn't there anyone who can come in and handle the office for you?" She didn't look too steady on her feet.

"Naw. I'm all set. There's a little sitting room and a daybed back there in case me and the mister get stranded in town."

When a long, wet cough rolled up from Barbara's chest, I decided the keys I was holding needed a good dousing in alcohol, or maybe bleach. My hand probably did, too.

"He'll be along when he gets out of work, and we're dead empty right now. Got a couple of reservations for the weekend, but I can be sick here as well as anywhere, I suppose."

It wasn't up to me to argue the logic, so I reminded her how often to take Leandra's cure and joined Patrea, who'd stayed back by the door. Probably to keep from being re-infected with the plague.

"You remember where the cleaning supplies are?" Mrs. Dexter called after me.

"In the closet behind the vending machines, right?"

I winced when she popped the top on the syrup bottle and drank at least two doses without measuring. "Yep," Barbara didn't even sniff when the syrup hit the back of her throat. "I really do appreciate the help."

Outside, Patrea turned a wide-eyed look my way. "How did she do that? There's enough alcohol in that stuff to choke a horse, and she just slugged it right down."

"What can I say? We small town women are made from sterner stuff."

"If she runs this place all by herself, I'd say she's made of steel."

While I unlocked the dark green door to get to the cleaning closet, I explained a little bit about how the town had suffered when the new road to Hackinaw bypassed Mooselick River. "The town lost a lot of revenue, and some of the smaller businesses that relied on tourists passing through, well, they're gone now."

One side of the closet held sheets and towels, the other a wheeled cart which we piled high with whatever we thought we'd need.

Patrea pushed the cart while I carried the vacuum cleaner. "Once the jobs went," I said, "people started moving away. It doesn't take long for a town this small to die. I've been helping an enthusiastic group of women try to bring it back from the brink."

"I suppose that's one way to use your skills. What's in it for you?"

That one question proved a certain amount of distance between us.

"The satisfaction of doing something productive with my time. Not having to watch my friends move away to find better jobs. Feeling useful." Annoyed, my tone sharpened. "Does everything have to be about money?"

The squeaking wheels went silent when Patrea stopped pushing the cart. "I do plenty of pro bono work. You should know that better than anyone. I wasn't talking about money at all. Hard as it is to believe, I do understand the satisfaction of doing something to help others."

I'd put my foot in my mouth that time. "I'm sorry, I truly am. That came off like a dig at you because I'm touchy on the subject of money. Please say you'll forgive me."

My heart settled back to a more normal rhythm because the smile she flashed looked sincere. "Of course," she said. "In my line of work, it pays to develop a thick skin. Mine is thicker than most. However, what I meant to ask was if you're considering looking for a job where you could use your unique set of skills."

I had unique skills?

"As what? I was a glorified party planner. Trust me, when I went to job services looking for work, my unique set of skills was not in high demand. I lucked into the job with Spencer and then took over for him as property manager for Leo when he died. My living expenses are low, and Leo pays pretty well, so I get by. I've selling off pieces of furniture at the shop for a little extra here and there, but I'm happy with my situation."

By unspoken agreement, we were starting in Amber's room first, so I bent to unlock the door as I talked. "And helping the town isn't a bad thing. I think we stand a chance to make it boom again."

The cart rattled up behind me. "Because we've had this discussion on more than one occasion, I'll refrain from pointing out that you're in this situation by choice, but there are other non-profit organizations that would have snapped you up in a hot minute."

"Really?" I turned and arched an eyebrow. "And what good would that have done me? Because you had to ride in like a knight in shining armor to defend my honor from Paul and his smear campaign. Don't think I'm unaware that he's after more than my reputation."

Turning the key, I pushed open the door.

"Hey, you forgot to do the discreet knock and say housekeeping," Patrea said. "That's the best part of this gig."

"You can do the next one." I shook my head at her odd sense of humor and continued our previous conversation. "I've had some time to think through the implications. The best way to keep me from dipping into his pockets is to get me out of the way. Since I can't see Paul resorting to murder, having me sent to prison for a crime I didn't commit would be the next best thing."

With that, I turned and felt for the light switch.

All thought of Paul and my legal issues dropped away when Patrea got her first look inside the motel room. "Holy retro kitsch, Batman." Her eyes rounded and so did her mouth. "I can't...I just...wow."

"It does sort of hit you in the face, doesn't it?"

Papered in geometric shapes in shades of olive and chocolate brown, the walls were the least jarring pattern in the room. That award would go to the carpeting in an orange and red stylized floral that threatened to make my eyes bleed and rendered Patrea fairly speechless.

A smile crept over my face as she continued to goggle. "The decor is part of the draw."

It took her a moment to shake off the inertia and look past the riot of color to notice the fine layer of fingerprint dust and other evidence of a police search. "I wonder if they found anything to help the investigation along."

"They got my tablet," A chill breeze alerted me to her presence a split second before Amber shivered into view. "My clothes, but not my purse or my phone. Those haven't turned up yet, and no, I don't know where they are."

None of what she said was an answer to Patrea's question, though, and in the narrow confines of the room, I couldn't just ask for more clarification, so I had to improvise. "I guess that depends on what she had in her personal effects. I'm assuming a laptop or tablet of some kind. Maybe there were threatening emails or she had compromising information on people that could make her a target."

Amber took the hint. "Oh, sure. I know plenty of secrets, but I've never been killed for any of them before."

I wanted, in my most sarcastic tone, to tell her she probably wouldn't be killed again, either, but I bit down on the comment to keep Patrea from doubting my sanity. I also wanted to ask Amber how she'd landed her job since she didn't strike me as the most balanced of personalities. Dead or alive; on air or not.

"It only takes one." Patrea shrugged, bundled up the garishly striped bedspread with the sheets that had also been tossed aside, presumably by the police during their search, and put them in the laundry bag hanging on the cleaning cart. "Looks like they did half our job for us, but they certainly didn't hold back with the fingerprinting powder. I thought that stuff would be obsolete by now. They never use it on TV anymore."

I fired up the vacuum cleaner, switched to the dusting attachment, and raised my voice to be heard over the whir and hum, "If there's a better way, it's probably not in the budget."

Still, we checked under the bed, and under the mattress as well as in the hidden mini-fridge for evidence. Other than the linens and the bible in the nightstand, there was nothing left in the room. Somewhere along the line, Amber faded out and didn't return. I guess we weren't entertaining enough for her—not that I cared. With her gone, there was less chance of bumping into or through her in the confined space.

A half hour saw the room shipshape and ready for the next guests. I noted with interest that Barbara had taken my suggestion about leaving information cards in the rooms.

"Let's skip over to seven next, and get the easiest one out of the way," Patrea said. I handed her the keys and let her do her housekeeping knock.

"That was fun."

"Your idea of fun and mine are a mile apart." When she went in, I pushed the cart close to the door and followed. I was looking down at a speck of lint on my shirt and plowed into Patrea's back. She'd frozen just inside the door. When I looked up to apologize, the *I'm sorry* fell right out of my head.

"What the hell happened in here?"

All I got was a wide-eyed look and a slow head shake. "Did she say little old ladies? Are you sure we heard right?"

The room looked like the aftermath of a hurricane and smelled like someone had dumped a bottle of whiskey into the bottom of a gym bag full of month-old socks. The mattress hung off the end of the bed by a couple of feet, the bedspread was gone, and the sheets were a knotted, filthy mess. Stuffing leaked from one of the pillows, the door to the mini fridge hung wide, and the shower curtain was balled up inside.

"Old ladies had themselves a party. What's the grandma equivalent of spring break?"

If I hadn't been the person in charge of cleaning up after them, I might have found more humor in the dry observation. As it was, I did the only thing I could think of at the moment, and pulled out my camera to snap a shot. No one would believe what we were looking at without proof. Then I went back to the cart to retrieve the most important things we would need.

In unison, we snapped on elbow length rubber gloves and set about cleaning up after Grandmas Gone Wild.

What happened during the next hour, the things we saw, the things we found, went into the vault never to be spoken of again. At the end of it, Patrea and I had shared one of those experiences that either cements or ends a friendship.

We looked shell-shocked and felt battle-weary when we closed the door to number seven behind us.

"That was—," Patrea lost the will to speak.

"Yep. It was."

Compared to seven, four was a walk in the park. The cameraman had left the bedspread folded neatly at the bottom of the bed, and the wet towels in a pile in the bathtub.

Because it was her turn—for eternity after I'd tackled the one in seven—Patrea took the bathroom while I stripped and remade the bed. I'd just tucked the sheet in at the top when I caught sight of something pink stuffed into one of the pillow cases.

As soon as my fingers touched silk and lace, I knew I'd hit on something important.

"Whoa, come check this out. I found something."

"Hey, those are my panties." If ghosts didn't stop popping in out of thin air, I was going to do…well, nothing because that's the only option I had.

"What did you—," Patrea stepped out of the bathroom at the same time the door to the room swung open.

"What a surprise," sarcasm dripped off Ernie Polk's tongue like molasses out of a jar. "Finding Everly Dupree at a crime scene. Because that never happens."

"Cut me a break." Slowly and deliberately, I slipped Amber's underwear into my pocket. "Mrs. Dexter's sick, and I'm just giving her a hand with the cleaning because my mother volunteered me for the job. I wasn't trolling for evidence."

Lie. Huge lie

"If you wanted to see a crime scene, you should have shown up when we were cleaning seven." Patrea's hazel eyes met Ernie's flat gaze and didn't waver. "What those two old ladies did to that room was positively criminal."

"Mrs. Dexter said you'd cleared the rooms for cleaning. I'm sorry if she made a mistake, but we're just about finished. If it helps, we didn't find anything important."

Another lie, and I told it without batting so much as an eyelash. My heartbeat kicked into overdrive, but Ernie couldn't tell, I didn't think. He waited a long moment to speak, and then told us there'd been no mistake.

"I stopped by to check on Barb, but now that you're here and handy, I have to ask, where were you between the hours of eleven am and two pm on the day of the murder?"

Had he followed me out here to accuse me of killing Amber?

"Why, is that the window you have for the time of death?" It had to be or he wouldn't have asked; I just wanted to hear him say it.

"Just answer the question."

"Amber rang my doorbell at ten am, the same as she'd done the two days prior. I've told you all of this already. On the advice of my lawyer," I gestured to Patrea, "I had decided to give a statement when Amber returned. We prepared said statement, then drove to Curated Collections to buy Patrea an outfit suitable for wearing on camera. Then we went back to my place, got dressed and waited."

Which put me in proximity of the scene of the crime during the time of death window.

"Did you see anyone else during that time? Or did anyone else see you leave the shop?"

What he meant was anyone who wouldn't lie for me, I'm sure.

"Geez, Ernie, if I'd known I was gonna need an alibi, I'd have looked around a little." My fingers clenched on Amber's panties. "I don't remember seeing anyone, but that's not to say no one was out and about. You do remember it was snowing, don't you?"

He continued to look at me.

"I could barely see across the street. What's your theory on my possible motive? That she was bothering me for an interview? If that was all it took, I'd have laid waste to a whole slew of people."

Ernie pinched the bridge of his nose as if a nagging headache lodged there. As much as he might be annoyed at me for landing in the middle of more than one murder investigation, I didn't really think Ernie considered me a suspect.

He didn't offer any reassurance that he believed me, but told us to carry on, and left.

"Weird," Patrea said when the door closed behind him. "Now what—," I shook my head and held a finger to my lips to stop her asking the obvious question. For all I knew, Ernie lurked outside to eavesdrop.

"—else is left to do? I'm done in there," She pointed a thumb over her shoulder. Patrea caught on quickly.

"Just finish making the bed, while I vacuum, and then drop off the dirty linens in the bin. If I remember correctly, there's a service that picks them up."

When we went outside, Ernie had gone.

Patrea waited until we were in the car and headed out of town before asking what I'd found. By that time, Amber had gone again, but she'd already told me about her tryst with Lance Colby.

Instead, we contented ourselves with speculation on our new prime suspect. The cameraman could be the killer. After all, weren't love, money, or revenge at the heart of most murders?

"Maybe sleeping with her would get him fired if people found out. Or maybe they got into a lover's quarrel that ended in death," Patrea drove as she did everything, with quiet competence. "After all, we did find her panties in his room."

Oddly enough, discussing murder helped settle my nerves down to only the occasional flare. For the several months since my marriage imploded, I'd maintained a careful perimeter around the ground zero center of that destruction. Going home with Patrea would put me well within the boundaries of an area I never wanted to visit again. Too many memories, both good and bad were attached to these places.

So, I concentrated on Amber and pushed thoughts of Paul and Reva out of my head. "I heard the cameraman talking on

79

the phone while I was waiting for you to come back of the shop the night Amber died. He was telling someone, I assume at the station, that he'd been trying to call her for hours and she wasn't picking up."

Sagely, Patrea nodded. "Establishing his alibi."

Lance Colby zoomed to the top of my list of suspects, and I made a mental note to ask Amber for more information about him the first chance I got.

Whether or not Ernie was looking seriously at me for the crime, I wanted this one solved before Christmas.

# CHAPTER 12

For all her love of antiques and old houses, Patrea lived in a thoroughly modern townhouse just inside the city limits. Not at all what I expected. After she unlocked the door, she turned, caught my surprised expression, and offered a throaty chuckle.

"Remodeling old houses is my passion, but this place will do until I find *the one*. Otherwise, I'd just end up moving every year, and I hate moving."

"That's valid. I'd hate to have to do it again." Especially given the sheer volume of stuff I now owned. It would take me a year just to pack. "But you're planning to stay in the area, right? I haven't really watched the housing market here, but I remember seeing homes for sale in the older neighborhoods sometimes."

Shrugging off her coat and tossing it over the arm of a vintage sofa—the interior, I could see right away, was furnished more to Patrea's tastes—she headed toward the stairs. "To tell you the truth, I'm not sure. If I found the right place, I don't think I'd have any trouble relocating. Make yourself at home, I'll just pack a bag and be right down."

Because she'd offered the invitation, I wandered around the open-concept kitchen and living space. Painted a neutral color somewhere between tan and gray, the walls reflected plenty of light to bounce and scatter off the polished surfaces of oak, walnut, and mahogany tables and shelves.

I picked up a framed photograph of Patrea. Fifteen, maybe sixteen, her hair a long mane that might have been the style of the day, but didn't suit her face. Still, she smiled at the camera—no, I corrected myself—past the camera at the person taking the photo. It was an unguarded moment, rare for the Patrea I knew. Sighing, I returned the photo to where I'd found it.

For her home, she'd chosen fabrics in warm, not too fussy patterns to balance out the hard edges. The whole place felt cozy and inviting. I'd already discovered the softer woman under the prickly exterior, and her home fit her like a glove.

"You have a beautiful home. Very restful."

"Thanks," Patrea gave me one of her rare smiles. "I still envy your place, though. All those lovely old things, and so much room to spread out."

"Hah," I snorted. "You say that because you're in the nice room. The one I cleaned, cleared, and banished the pack-rat from right before the yard sale." It had been a few months since then, and I'd confined my efforts to sorting out the downstairs rooms and trying to make a dent in Catherine's secret garret in the addition. "The infestation has not been fully exterminated. Maybe I should let you loose in one of the other bedrooms. See if you start singing another tune."

I meant it as a threat, but Patrea took it as a promised treat. Just goes to show how different people are under the skin.

With just enough time left before my clandestine operation to accost Albert in the parking lot, we stopped for subs on the way there and sat with the motor running while we ate and watched for him to come out. Just before he was due, I checked for his car. Something I should have done first, by the way, because it wasn't there.

"Should I go in? What if someone sees me?" That would be bad. "You do it."

"He's not going to talk to me, it has to be you. You're the one he likes." Patrea drummed her fingers on the steering wheel. "You don't have to go in, though. Just wait outside for him, right?"

"I guess."

"Okay, here's what we'll do. Swap coats with me, and I've got some sunglasses in the glove box." She wasn't satisfied until my hair was tucked under my hat. "Your own mother wouldn't know you now."

Patrea's coat fell most of the way to my knees, and I looked like a little girl playing dress up, but she was right, I didn't look like me anymore.

"Now go, before you miss him." I can't say I appreciated the shove but it did get me going with five minutes to spare. I spent those five minutes and the next five besides, pretending to take a phone call while leaning against a lamp post outside my former office and watching for Albert.

When he didn't come out, I waited five more, until Patrea pulled up to the curb and let down the window. "What's going on?"

"I don't know. Maybe he's working overtime."

"Just go in. No one will recognize you, and I'm getting cold just listening to your teeth chatter."

I thought about it for a moment. "I suppose I could. No one has gone in or out the whole time I've been standing here. Which is odd now that I think about it. I had some holiday functions set up ahead, so the place should be hopping right about now."

That it wasn't made me curious, and so I sucked up the nervous spit pooling in my mouth and went inside. Not only wasn't Albert there, a man I didn't recognize sat at his station. Worse, Amber stood between me and him, arms folded, waiting. Why couldn't she have come outside while I was standing around alone? Because it was more fun to jabber at me when I couldn't answer. I swear she took some perverse pleasure in doing that. She must have taken my warning glance to heart, because she stayed quiet for once.

"Excuse me," I lowered my voice an octave and said to the new guy, James, according to his name tag, "Is Albert here? I came by to wish him a Merry Christmas. He usually works on Wednesdays."

83

James never twitched so much as an eyebrow. "I work on Wednesdays."

"So I see. Did Albert change shifts? Will he be in tomorrow?"

"Ma'am," James finally looked up at me, his gaze as bored as his voice. "I work days, Dante works nights. Got a guy comes in on weekends, but his name isn't Albert."

"Okay, then. Well, you have a nice Christmas."

Amber followed me out. "I have news."

"You have under a minute before I get in the car. Give me the abridged version."

She did, with a side order of dirty look.

"The offices are empty. All of them. Cleaned out. The only person James is guarding is the receptionist, and I heard her telling someone on the phone that all events through the end of the December were canceled, and no, she didn't have a schedule of activities for January or February."

"All events?" My heart sank. "Even the special Santa visits?" If there was one thing I'd loved about my work it was Santa delivering toys to kids who might not otherwise have a Christmas.

"I only know what I heard and saw. She said all events, and the offices are cleared out. No plants, no photos on the desks, no printers, shredders, file cabinets, computers. Nothing."

"Thanks. We need to talk again later." Patrea had been idling two buildings down, and when she saw me pulled ahead so I could slide into the passenger's seat.

"Well?" She said as I stashed her sunglasses back in the glove box and flinched at the static flickering around my head when I pulled off the knit cap to let my hair tumble back down. "Was he in there? What did you find out?"

"Gone." With sharp motions, I snapped the seatbelt into the receptacle. "Fired or quit, I'm not sure which. Probably because of me."

84

Patrea spared me a look, pulled away from the curb, and went left at the end of the street instead of right to get on the highway. "Where are we going?" I said, though the dread settling in the pit of my stomach seemed to know already.

"Put your hat and glasses back on," was all she said, but I knew the way to my former home and once she made the next right turn, there was no doubt we were about to cruise past it.

I can't say what I was expecting to see, but nothing— well, other than the for sale sign planted in the snowbank— seemed different. Slowing, Patrea did what I suspect she'd have asked me to do if my fingers hadn't been shaking, and took a photo of the sign.

Maybe I was too close to the situation to see what she was seeing, because she nodded and said, "Of course."

I didn't say anything else until we were back on the road and headed home.

"There's no one left at the offices except the receptionist and security. Everything's closed down and empty." I let Patrea assume I'd asked a few questions.

She didn't seem surprised. "Probably seized in the investigation."

"I hate this. They canceled everything. The Christmas gala, the Santa visits. Months of my work, thousands and thousands of dollars meant to shelter the homeless this winter, to put smiles on the faces of kids when Santa handed them just the right thing." Fury burned in me at the waste of it all. So many who counted on help this time of year would now go without and there was nothing I could do about it.

Except there was.

"Turn around. Right now."

"What? Why?" Patrea slowed, and when I told her who I wanted to see, and why, did as I asked. With a smile, no less.

We did switch our coats back before making unexpected visits to three of the donors to past projects that I thought were neutral enough not to shut me out, but I can't say we looked anything like professionals while doing so. And maybe that

85

was in our favor. But at the end of the day, after bulling our way into two offices and a private home, we'd arranged for some of the lost money to be sent where it was needed.

Jacy had graciously agreed to let Molly out and feed her because it was past dark when we pulled back into town, but at least we returned in triumph. The kind of triumph that demanded pizza.

Even though I'd called ahead, there was a ten-minute wait at the counter, during which time Patrea grumbled a little. "I know it's a small town, but shouldn't they still offer delivery?"

"They do, I don't." It only takes one homicidal maniac on your front steps with a pizza box to put you off the concept for life. Trust me on that.

By the time we were settled on the sofa, with the half empty box on the coffee table and Molly gently accepting a piece of crust from her fingertips, she'd forgotten why she was annoyed.

"What do they put in this sauce?" Patrea licked a smudge of it from her index finger. "It's divine."

"Magic pixie dust, I think. It's a super-secret special recipe, you can't even get it unless you're in the know, and I'm fairly certain it's addictive."

I'd certainly eaten plenty of it since I'd moved home. Barring the two months I'd sworn off the place entirely, but I eventually reasoned out that my attacker was safely in jail, and why should I punish my taste buds for his actions?

By tacit agreement, we didn't talk about the events of the day, and I agreed let Patrea pick the movie. Amber, I hoped, would show up later, but for the next two hours, I planned to snuggle my dog and let Hallmark take me away.

Still tuned to channel five, we caught a glimpse of the news when Patrea turned on the television. Mia, the reporter who'd shown up on my doorstep after Amber's death, flicked a lock of blond hair over her shoulder. The cut and color matched her predecessors so closely I had to do a double take to make sure I wasn't seeing the image of Amber's ghost on screen.

"...Gregory Gilbert, the injured man, says he was trying to buy his daughter a My Magic Pony Dream House when he was nearly trampled by a crowd of other shoppers," Mia intoned, a wide smile on her face that made it seem as though she was pleased rather than concerned for the poor guy.

Her co-anchor, who seemed to feel the same way I did, faltered slightly and cast her a narrow-eyed look before saying, "Mr. Gilbert has been released from the hospital after being treated for minor wounds. We at channel five wish him a speedy recovery, and we'd like to remind everyone to be careful when you're out shopping. It can get pretty scary out there."

Yeah, he wasn't kidding.

# CHAPTER 13

"Well, hello. Glad you finally bothered to show up." Amber lounged on my bed. Or at least she hovered over it. Molly took one look at the ghost, then tilted her head for another before settling down in her bed. At least she'd quit growling every time Amber showed up.

"I've had a long day, and very little of it was fun. I appreciate your patience, though." All I wanted to do was crawl under the covers, but not with her. The sensation of human flesh meeting ghostly...um...not-flesh, was not one I preferred to repeat any more than necessary.

Before I had a chance to say a word Amber quirked an eyebrow and said, "Your ex is never going to sell that house, you know."

"Maybe not this minute, but the market usually picks up in January. It's a beautiful house in a good area. He shouldn't have any trouble."

If anything, Amber's brow went higher. "Really? Your definition of beautiful and mine don't run along the same lines, then. This place is old, but it's not so bad. That one is a hot mess."

"Well, I know the minimalist interior design isn't for everyone, and to be totally honest, it wasn't for me, but I wouldn't go so far as to call it a hot mess."

Incredulity turned to a frown as Amber thought for a moment. "So you like purple and gray?"

Now my brows were the ones shooting upward. Clearly, we were talking at cross purposes. "Purple? And gray?" Since this looked like it would take a while, I settled into the chair at my desk.

"It's funny, I didn't take you for being that tacky."

I shook my head and tried again. "When I lived in that house, the interior was white. Like white on white, even. With a few touches of something that could almost be called gray. The whole place felt sterile because he wouldn't allow so much as a pop of color in the pillows or throws."

Amber shrugged, "I guess his tastes have changed."

Of course. He was with Reva now. I wasn't sure what tweaked at the sore places I thought had healed the most—that he'd never let me change anything, or that he'd let her have carte blanch. Still, Amber was right. He wasn't going to sell that house anytime soon if it looked like the interior had been designed by Bimbos 'R Us.

Sue me if I took a little satisfaction in Paul's misfortune. What's more, I didn't even feel guilty about it.

"Wait." More questions popped into my head. "You went inside. Why?"

Another shrug. "I'm curious by nature. It's what made me so good at my job."

Everyone should play to their strengths, I supposed.

"Was she there?" I both wanted and didn't want to know. "Never mind, I really don't want to know." Another thought occurred. "Can you go wherever you want, whenever you want? Or only to places you've been before?"

The question seemed to surprise because Amber looked nonplussed. "I guess I haven't really tried to go someplace new." Promptly, she squinched up her face and poofed. You'd think I'd have taken over the bed the second she was gone, but I worried she might return in the same spot, and I was right. Not even a minute later, she was back.

"Only places I've been. Kind of a bummer, I was hoping to take in Paris before I blew this Popsicle stand." Then she gave me a cheeky grin, "Still, since I'm attached to you, I can follow you anywhere like I did to your ex's house today.

Fancy a trip to Paris? I'd be great company, and you wouldn't even have to buy me a ticket."

"No, but I'd have to buy me one, and that's not in the budget."

Eyes narrowing, Amber made a pfft sound. "Even with the pre-nup, you must have found a way to squirrel away something for a rainy day."

I didn't want to talk about money with Amber, but she kept at me until it was either give in or go sleep on the couch and try to explain that to Patrea in the morning.

"Look, I know you think I'm an idiot. On some fronts, I wouldn't disagree with you, but I trusted my husband until he showed me I couldn't, and that was the last time I saw him. Not very modern of me, but there you go. If I hadn't been a blind fool, then maybe I'd have…no, you know what? I probably wouldn't have done anything different."

There was a pause before Amber, in a quieter tone than I'd heard her use before, said, "I stopped trusting people when I was six. My mother left for the weekend and said she'd be back on Monday, but she wasn't. She'd taken all her clothes. My father insisted she'd come back to us, but she never did. I lost faith in him for not keeping his word. In her for taking off and leaving me alone. In everyone, really."

"I'm sorry." I said it simply, and meant it with all my heart.

As if embarrassed by her moment of true confession, Amber waved away my sympathy and grinned.

"I guess you could say I turned my greatest flaw into my biggest asset with my job. Not trusting people and having a curious mind made me good at probing for details."

Look how much she'd persuaded me to admit.

"Maybe so, but those things could also be what got you killed," I reminded her.

"Probably."

Amber didn't seem terribly broken up about being dead, or for that matter deeply motivated to find out who killed her.

I wanted to ask why, but it was getting late and I wanted sleep more. "Tell me about the cameraman. I assume you were intimate with him, or was he the kind of creeper who steals a woman's panties and sleeps with them under his pillow?"

Grinning cheerfully, she waggled her eyebrows at me. "He could be, but in this case, they probably ended up down behind there when he tossed me on the bed. Hidden depths, that one. But you know, I plumbed them all, or let him plumb mine."

I didn't really want to talk about his or Amber's plumbing. "So you were dating?"

As loud as Amber hooted, I was glad Patrea couldn't hear her. "Dating? No, we were not doing that. Doing plenty of other stuff, but I wouldn't call any of it dating."

"For how long?" Even the casual relationship she alluded to could be a reason for her death if he wanted more than she did.

"Oh honey, he could go all night."

Too much information. Just way too much. My brain suggested I put my fingers in my ears and sing the *lalalala I can't hear you* song. But that wouldn't get Amber into the light. "Ew," I said instead.

"You know what I meant."

"Well, you weren't being subtle." Idly, I used my toe to spin my chair back and forth. "Still, I need to ask him a few questions. Give me his phone number."

Bless her heart, she certainly tried, and then cursed at finding that piece of information no longer in her memory.

"Okay," I rose and headed toward the bathroom to change. "I'm running on fumes. We'll talk more tomorrow." Turning back, I asked the question that had just jumped to mind. "Where do you go when you're not here?"

After a pause, Amber answered. "I go home and sit with my dad. He's not doing so well with all of this, and I like to think he can feel me there. Like my presence is comforting."

91

When Amber faded, she left behind an ineffable sadness that had me, just for a moment, reconsidering my stance on messages to loved ones.

The feeling lasted into the night, and even after I let Molly up for a cuddle on the bed. I tossed and turned until she decided her bed was preferable to being kicked again. Finally, I flicked the light back on and looked for something to read. A good book might take my mind off the morass of images in my head.

Paul. Paul and Reva. Purple and gray. Empty offices. Amber and the cameraman. They scrolled past in an endless loop.

I searched the shelf, but nothing seemed to pull my interest until I remembered Catherine's diaries. I'd found them during a fit of clearing out her things and stashed them in my night stand for later perusal.

The previous owner of my house had lived a secret life once her husband passed. She'd added rooms onto the place and installed a rat's warren of garrets for various pursuits during her remaining years" pottery, painting, collecting and re-purposing furniture into art installations. More collecting than re-purposing.

Over the past couple of months, I'd cleared some space back there and sent a number of pieces to Jacy and Neena to sell at Curated Collections for a little extra cash. They'd done well by me, garnering almost as much, even with their cut of the profits, as I could have sold the pieces at auction.

What Catherine would think of my actions, I had no idea, but I hoped she'd look upon them with benevolence because something had to give. The addition practically groaned under the weight of her addiction for things. Nice things, mind you, but still too many.

Curious to know my strange benefactor better, I pulled out a diary at random, flipped through a few pages until a passage caught my eye, and began to read.

*Why must people feel the need to push men in my direction? Worse, how do they assume I can't see past the hopeful smiles as they introduce their widowed brother or uncle or father. It's beyond the pale. I've had my love and my lifetime with him, short as it was, was enough. I'm quite happy here with my things, and I'm too old for fluttering hearts or adjusting my ways to make room for someone else,* she wrote.

Paul hadn't been the love of my life, which would have been nice to figure out before I married him, but everyone makes mistakes. Now, with some distance, I saw how it had all played out. How I'd been addle-headed enough to let him sweep me off my feet—and yes, it burned that my mother called that one—into a marriage that wasn't right for me. Worse, one that slowly turned into a cage.

Maybe I didn't need to know why Paul had picked me, and I probably never would. Here, in the house of Catherine, I would heal. Had already. Mostly.

If nothing else, today had proved I was in a better place.

Yet, Catherine had a point. I wasn't sure when or if I would be ready to make room in my life for someone else. Or if I could ever trust my judgment again. Amber's little talk on trust hit home in unexpected ways. Did I want to end up like her?

With all those thoughts in my head, I went back to reading.

*Yet, the house echoes with emptiness, and the regret that we were never blessed with children when we'd hoped for a passel. The nursery sits as barren as my womb, and I find myself drawn to stand outside that door and mourn the little lives that were never mine.*

*How easy it would be to follow Basil into that good night. A few of the pills my doctor has pressed upon me to help me sleep, and I could. The endless sleep. It calls to me with seductive whispers and dreams of my love.*

*It's not in me to take the easy way. No, I won't succumb to temptation, and will do as I promised my dear, sweet Basil. I will live for him while he cannot, and join him when my time is come, though my desolate heart lay broken and bleeding even still. I fear it shall never heal.*

Okay, if I hadn't been certain before, reading of Catherine's great love for Basil proved my feelings for Paul a shadow of what hers had been, and certainly not enough to contemplate dying over. Checking the date, I saw she'd written these words over a year after Basil's death. I sighed for her, and because there was more in the same vein, flipped ahead and kept reading.

*Sometimes, I feel phantom hands upon mine as the clay whirls and spins, as I shape it between palms roughened by the silt and grit hidden within the deceptively yielding softness. Basil would have loved throwing clay, the primal joy in building up a wall, the delicate touch that shapes and molds one thing into another. The trial by fire in the kiln. Will the center hold? Or will it shatter into shards?*

*There is that within me as well. A fire that burns to create, and to build, and to make. It is a fever, and maybe an addiction, but the fire burns clean, and I feel reborn as the phoenix from the flame.*

Catherine's words stirred a desire in me to create something new for myself. What that might be, I had no idea, but I wanted to feel reborn. If she could do it...why couldn't I?

# CHAPTER 14

The scents of cinnamon and ginger and sugar woke me the next morning. A glance at the clock through slitted lids told me I'd overslept. Why hadn't Molly made a peep? She'd been slowly adjusting to my sleep schedule, but by now, she'd have been doing her gotta pee walk between the bed and the door. Even I couldn't sleep through that.

She wasn't in her bed, and it took me a few seconds to realize Patrea must have let the dog out and given me a chance to sleep in. For that, I might just have to kiss her.

Well, for that and for whatever it was she was doing that made the house smell like a bakery. If there was fresh coffee in the pot, she'd get a hug, too.

I heard Christmas carols playing in the kitchen and directed my slippered feet in that direction.

Two steps inside the door, I froze and tried to take in the scene before me.

First, Patrea was wearing candy cane striped pajamas under a poinsettia patterned apron she'd unearthed from the collection I'd left in the drawer where Catherine kept them. Second, it looked like she'd been baking for hours.

"What's all this?"

The grin took a couple of years off Patrea's face; she should smile like that more often. "It's all your fault. You and your hometown Christmas. I've got the baking bug, and when I'm done here, we're going to decorate a tree. There will be hot chocolate, and music, and you're rigging up the lights. I hate that part."

"I hadn't planned on having a tree since I was doing Christmas day with my folks." There was coffee, and I selected an over-sized mug because I figured I'd need it to keep up with Patrea. "It's probably too late to get one this close to the big day and all."

Patrea waved a wooden spoon in my direction. "There will be a tree somewhere in this town, and if I can't find it, I'll go sneak into the woods and cut one down. You promised me a Christmas experience, and I'm wringing every drop of yuletide cheer out of it if it kills me."

That phrase probably wasn't the best one to use around me, but I didn't think Patrea was in any danger of dying.

"A tree sounds nice, and since I only have a few decorations of my own, we'll use the ones that came with the house." Digging them out would give Patrea a look behind the addition door. Knowing her, she'd see that as a treat. "Cathcrine Willowby collected Christmas decorations with about the same fervor she collected everything else. Halloween, too, though I didn't find them until it was too late this year. "

Opting not to put up a tree, I'd still pulled out quite an array of decorations to make the house look festive, but I didn't tell Patrea that digging through Cathcrine's things creeped me out a little. Not because it felt wrong to sort through a stranger's belongings—I'd finally pushed past that—but because our tastes ran so similar it was as if she'd chosen every item with me in mind.

Granted, I might not have opted for the volume my benefactor seemed to crave, but then again, sorting through some of her things felt a little like shopping in a store personalized just for me. Not all of them, mind you, but enough that I wasn't always sure how to feel about the experience.

"That's settled, then. Grab a slice of panettone, and we'll go pick out a tree right now." The redoubtable Patrea clapped her hands in such delight I beamed a smile at her. Putting up a tree would be fun. "I'll just pop this dough in the fridge to proof slowly, and we'll have brioche for breakfast."

"We'll have to take your car, and strap the tree to the roof," I warned, and she waved a hand at me as though a needle scratch or two on her paint was no big deal. "And we'll have to take Molly or she might decide to sample your wares. So far, she's never touched anything on the table, but this is an awful lot of temptation.

Still carrying my coffee, I strolled around the room to look at what she'd made. "There's three kinds of fudge here. How long have you been up?"

"Since before the sun, but fudge is easy. Those two kinds use the same base, so I doubled the recipe, then divided the batch and beat in the final flavors at the end. Helps to be ambidextrous so you can stir two bowls at once."

"My butt is getting bigger just from the proximity."

"Well, get dressed before all your pants stop fitting." Patrea tossed the cheery comment over her shoulder as she headed down the hall toward the stairs. "I need five minutes to get dressed and ten to put things away in the kitchen." The implication was that I'd better be ready. Once she set her mind to a task, the woman wasted no time getting started.

True to her word, she was back downstairs in ten, and in fifteen we were cruising past the nearly empty tree corral that had been set up in one corner of the grocery store parking lot.

"Well, there's one left." It was turning orange around the edges and looked like it might shed most of its needles if we tried to pick it up. "But it doesn't look good."

"Okay, what's our next option?"

I thought for a minute. "There used to be a place out toward the lake where you could cut your own. I haven't been out that way since snow fell, and I didn't pay much attention before then, so it might or might not be open."

A song came on the radio about an unfortunate reindeer accident involving a grandmother as we drove, and when Patrea started singing along, I joined in. I hadn't felt this light in my soul for weeks. She probably hadn't, either, given the way she'd taken on what hung over my head.

The drive to the lake wasn't long, but where trees shaded the road, snow built up in ridges and tracks, making it wise to drive slower, and there was no sun today in any case. Only a sky in shades of gray and blue bands. Partway out, a thin snow began to drift lazily down on the breeze.

"Forecast call for a storm?" Patrea twisted the radio dial looking for a station playing the news, and found one just in time to catch a forecast of occasional flurries.

"Guess not," I said, and pointed toward a break in the clouds. "Looks like it'll pass. We're almost there, anyway." Just as I made the observation, the sign for the farm came into view. "That's the place. Evergreen Farm."

Despite the lowering sky and the spitting snow, Patrea grinned. "I've never cut down a tree before. This is going to be fun."

Half an hour later, while she huffed and puffed and dragged a bow-shaped saw against a reluctant tree trunk, optimism had flown out the window along with ladylike language.

"Hey, you are the one who decided you had to cut your own. I'd have been happy to pick one of the stragglers from the lot."

My comment earned me a dirty look as Patrea started to swear again, "Son of a—,"

"You're going about it all wrong." A male voice interrupted Patrea's tirade, and she stood abruptly. From my position on the opposite side of the tree, I saw it all happen. Surprised, since neither of us had heard anyone coming, Patrea took a step back and tangled her feet together. The saw went up and over, but the man who owned the annoyed voice caught her on her way down.

Just like she'd requested, save for the fact that she hadn't fallen because of high heels, but the man's attitude fit the part.

He didn't seem at all impressed with her practically landing at his feet.

"Whoa there, missy."

Now, I firmly believe any man who calls a woman missy ought to be wearing a cowboy hat, have arms the size of tree trunks, and a smile brimming with charm above a chiseled chin. Otherwise, missy comes off as a slur, and even then, it could go either way.

Tall, dark, and hairy here, well, he missed the mark some. Substitute a knitted toque for the cowboy hat, and forget about the smile. Plus I couldn't tell about the chin because of his beard, but he did have the arms. Oh, boy, did he.

He set Patrea back on her feet, bent to retrieve the saw, handed it back and then, without introducing himself, offered a lecture—every word of it rife with the inference that we couldn't handle it on our own—on the proper technique of sawing through a spruce trunk.

"Here, give me that saw, I'll do it for you."

Snatching her hand behind her back, Patrea stood her ground. "I believe the sign says cut your own tree, which is an experience I don't intend to miss. Now, tell me again, what was I doing wrong?"

Disarmed by her even, almost cheerful tone, the man finally looked at Patrea full in the face.

"Hold the saw perpendicular to the trunk, not at an angle."

I might as well have ceased to exist for all the attention paid to me, but I didn't care because I found it fascinating to watch these two prickly people interact.

"Patrea Heard," she introduced herself, "and you are?"

"Chris. Chris Evergreen. This used to be my father's farm. It's mine now."

As tall as he was, he barely topped Patrea by an inch or two, so the pair stood almost eye-to-eye. "Well, Chris Evergreen, you've done yourself proud, now let's get me a tree."

There were no more outbursts from Chris as it was quite obvious his pique had no effect on Patrea's determination to cut her own tree, drag it from the woods, and haul it home. What he wouldn't see, and I did, but only because I'd watched enough romance movies with her was the tension in her body, the way it responded to his every movement as he put his hands over hers and showed her the right way to hold the saw.

The two of them made a picture amid a swirl of snowflakes, and I was pretty sure they'd forgotten all about me after a moment or two. A quick study, she got the hang of the motion in no time, and the tree began to tip.

"Catch it before it falls in the snow, or you'll need an extra day of drying time before you can put it up," Chris was talking to me, so I jumped to do as he said, and got a faceful of needles for my efforts. "You're lucky," he said, "it's been mostly sunny the past few days and we had that windy day that cleared off the snow. If you get this inside right away, it should dry out enough to decorate by this evening." The implication being we'd left things fairly late already.

I didn't get a good grip and almost dropped the tree, but managed to hang on and struggled to set it to rights. Patrea had almost sawed through.

"Hold it higher," Chris said, "it's binding the saw."

Heavier than I thought it would be, I wasn't ready to take the full weight of the tree, and Chris had to move fast to catch it before I dropped it into the snow.

"Thanks for your help, we've got it from here," Patrea handed Chris the saw and lifted the trunk. She took off, her longer legs making her speed a fair clip, leaving me to struggle along behind holding up the other end. I managed a few steps before Chris took pity on me. Leather glove-clad hands closed over the prickly top, and I let go with relief and trailed behind the pair of them all the way back to the Christmas tree lot.

Chris gave us a discount on the tree, he said because we were last-minute shoppers, but I suspected that was only part of the reason. He didn't say much else, though, while he wrapped the branches up with twine and helped tie it to the roof of the car. Neither did Patrea. No wonder she wasn't getting anywhere in the romance department.

I knew she was interested, but she didn't give Chris so much as a hint, so I risked her wrath and stuck my nose squarely into the middle of her business.

"We'll be out at the tavern tomorrow night. If you're not doing anything, stop in and we'll buy you a beer."

He gave me a nod, but didn't commit, and I figured I'd done all I could do. The rest was up to them. On the way home, I tried to broach the subject with Patrea, but she wasn't having any of it, so I chattered away about nothing while she said little.

We'd wrestled the tree off the roof and had it halfway through the front door when Ernie Polk pulled his cruiser into the drive. He wasted no time making his way onto the porch, and when I caught a look at his grim expression, my knees turned to water.

# CHAPTER 15

"What's wrong? My parents?"

"They're fine. Everly, I need you to come down to the station and answer some questions. In an official capacity."

"Don't say a word." Patrea ordered before I could open my mouth. "I'm Miss Dupree's attorney. What are the charges?"

"Did I say I was charging her with anything?"

"It's okay, Patrea. Ernie, what's this about? I told you everything I know about Amber Hale. I'm not sure what else I'd have to say that can help." Maybe I'd left a few things out, but really, what little I did know wouldn't help. I knew Amber had come to town hoping to interview me, that she'd interviewed Paul, who had slurred my name up down and sideways, that she'd slept with her cameraman and danced with Chris Evergreen. And that she was dead, of course, but I didn't think Ernie could handle the whole truth. Not when it included the ghost herself shimmering into view behind him.

Running stumpy fingers through his brush cut hair, Ernie sighed. "I've got the feds on their way here, and they asked me to escort you to the station for a chat about your ex-husband. You can bring your lawyer, and you should." Molly nudged out past the tree that was still halfway in the door and leaned up against Ernie's leg. Absently, he reached down to pet her silky head and sighed.

"Look, Everly, I give you a hard time because you're constantly in my way, but I don't think you're the kind of person who would cheat needy people to line your own pockets."

That, coming from Ernie, was high praise indeed. Especially considering I'd helped put his sister in jail, but at least he didn't hold a grudge.

"I'm not, and I'm not sure how much help I'm going to be to the FBI, either. I didn't have anything to do with the financial side of things."

"Stop talking," Patrea's voice cut through the air. "Help me get this tree inside, and then we'll follow your friend here down to the station where I will do the talking and you will let me do my job. Am I clear?"

"Loud and."

While he worked mostly in Mooselick Falls, Ernie's office was located with the county police, and it was to that station we followed him. During the fifteen-minute ride, Patrea went over her strategy, which mainly consisted of my not offering any information, and her doing most of the talking.

"Stick to yes or no whenever possible, only elaborate when necessary, and watch for my signals."

My insides were jumping like a drop of water on a hot griddle.

Ernie led us to an interrogation room with a metal-topped table and some uncomfortable wooden chairs where a man and a woman already waited.

"I'm Special Agent Blake Sully," the man introduced himself and his partner, "and this is Special Agent Martine Coville." His lips curved into a smile, but no one told his eyes so they remained cold as he indicated we should take a seat. When Ernie introduced me and listed Patrea as my attorney of record, then also pulled up a chair, Sully gave him the same look.

"We can take it from here, officer Polk."

"I believe I'll stay." Ernie's tone was mild, but he didn't look to be going anywhere and since he'd settled on my side of the table, I thought his point was clear. I felt safer having him on my side.

"First," SA Coville took over, her face more relaxed than her partner's, "the bureau thanks you for your cooperation. Now, we'd like to ask you a few questions."

Patrea had warned me how this would go, and it seemed she'd been right when the first few questions were easy ones establishing my relationship, both former and present, with Paul and his family, and then my position within the company.

"I planned, and then managed events and functions with the purpose of raising funds for various charities." This was the statement Patrea had laid out.

"You spent a lot of money on those events, is that correct? How did you access those funds?"

I caught Patrea's subtle nod, and answered. "All expenses were invoiced. All invoices went directly to accounting to be paid."

"But you must have had some kind of expense account for wining and dining potential donors."

"That type of activity did not fall under my client's purview." Patrea's answer seemed to shock Sully, but not in a good way.

"Your client," he said with a hint of a sneer, "was listed as the Director of Fundraising in the company records. I should think that title would indicate the scope of her purview covered all fundraising activities, including private meetings with donors. Meetings for which Mrs. Hastings would surely foot the bill."

"No," I ignored Patrea's shut up signal, "I didn't have an expense account or a company credit card, because I never needed one."

"You didn't think that was odd? In your position, I mean." Coville's tone was gentler, but still probing as she played good cop to Sully's bad cop routine.

"Well, I do now, but at the time, it never came up. Paul or one of the family would have met with potential donors if there was a need, while I hosted events. Some for the donors for the purpose of raising money; some for recipients. Like right now, there would be a series of Santa visits to various organizations to deliver gifts to children who needed them."

Patrea jammed the heel of her boot down on my toe as the next question came fast and hard.

"And how did you pay for those gifts? Credit or debit?" This from Sully.

"They were donated, and before you ask, the Santas were all volunteers. Paul's mother always came with a carload of things, and I don't know how she paid for those either. Let me just say this once and then you can stop asking. I didn't handle the money. Not one penny, not ever. There were accountants for that. Maybe you should question them instead of me."

Coville flipped open the folder that had been lying on the table between us, spun it around, and shoved it over so I could see the top sheet of paper. It looked like an application for a bank account with my name on it. Reaching out, Patrea slid the folder closer to her and looked at me with the obvious question in her eyes. I shook my head, and finally did as she'd told me to do. I shut my mouth and let her do the talking. Ernie hadn't said a word the entire time, and since he was off to Patrea's left, I couldn't see his reaction.

"This is a fishing expedition, and it stops now. This," Patrea closed the folder and shoved it across the table, "doesn't prove my client had anything to do with the dispersal of restricted funds."

"This," Sully laid a hand over the folder, "is the tip of the iceberg. It proves she's been lying to us since she came in here."

I sucked in a breath to retort and took an elbow jab to the arm from Patrea, so I let it out on a sigh while she leaned back in her seat and narrowed her eyes. After a long moment, she pinned her gaze on Sully. "Are you looking for the real truth or the convenient one that Paul Hastings has served you up on a platter?"

105

"I'm looking for whoever has been misappropriating funds and laundering money. Right now, that looks like your client."

"Fine." Patrea leaned down and pulled out a folder from the bag she carried. "This is a report from a verifiable expert—one your agency uses, by the way—stating that in his opinion, Paul Hastings forged Everly Dupree's initials and signature on an addendum to the prenuptial agreement she signed." Patrea selected a sheet and spun it across the table. "It is also this expert's opinion that the forgery took place shortly before Hastings filed for divorce."

Sully's face went blank as he scanned the document, then handed it over to Coville.

"What did Hastings stand to gain from the addendum?" Sully dropped at least two levels on the sneer meter.

"That's just it, you see. He gained nothing. Miss Dupree received a minor inheritance from her aunt, which, according to the addendum, Hastings could have claimed half of, but he chose not to take the money. The addendum covered assets acquired during the marriage."

"Why go to the effort of forging documents if he wasn't going to follow through?" Ernie finally spoke.

"That's the big question, isn't it? There aren't many reasonable answers, which leads me to believe this might not be the only documents with her signature forged."

While Sully tapped his fingers on the table, Patrea added, "We're happy to submit more handwriting samples, but I believe if you send that account application to my expert, he'll be willing to testify it's a forgery as well. The only thing Everly Dupree is guilty of is marrying the wrong man."

I could have done without the emphatic delivery, because the bald statement made me sound like an idiot. But then, I felt like one, so whatever. I offered my full cooperation to the FBI and with Patrea's permission, told them everything I knew about how the Hastings family ran their charitable arm, which wasn't nearly enough.

By the time we left the police station it was coming on toward time for dinner, and I had a throbbing headache. I hit the button to power up the heated seat and waited for the warmth to wipe away some of the miserable tension settling into my lower back.

How had I not seen Paul for what he was? My mother had pegged him as a wrong one right from the beginning, but only in the context of not being good marriage material. Even she couldn't have seen this coming. Could she? Or had I been the only one taken in by Paul's charm?

"Everly!" Patrea nearly shouted my name.

"Sorry, what?"

"Snap out of it. This is no time to fall into a funk."

A tear gathered in the corner of my eye, but before it fell, I turned my head away and lost myself in thoughts of failure and the view out the window. When I finally came back from the maudlin place, I was alone in the car, parked in front of Bertino's.

*Snap to it, girl.* My grandmother's voice threaded through my head as it did during moments of stress. *You gonna let a man take your thunder? You're a Dupree, now buck up and start acting like it.*

Good advice, as always. Grammie Dupree never let anyone get her down. Right up until the end, she was a firecracker.

The scent of spicy sauce teased its way through the vents, and set my stomach rumbling with hunger.

"You back?" Patrea asked as she slid two boxes into the back seat and settled a bag beside them.

"I guess. Sorry, had some thinking to do. How bad is it?"

"It better not be bad." She deliberately mistook my intent. "You've got me hooked on that sauce and there's something different about the pepperoni. I might be tempted to move here just for the pizza."

107

She wasn't serious, but I wouldn't have minded if she were. "They make their own sausage, too." It couldn't hurt to sweeten the pot.

"I know. That little old woman in there could sell heat to a volcano. She told me about the sausage, then gave me a sample. I ended up buying a half hot/half sweet with peppers and onions to go along with the pepperoni."

Smiling because I'd been in the same boat before, I said, "Mrs. Petrakis is a hard woman to turn down. She's got that cute little face, and those twinkly eyes, and that adorable accent. Then she hits you with the soft sell and you're sunk. What else did she talk you into?"

"Nothing," Patrea lied.

I sniffed at the scents coming from the bag. "You bought Baklava and bread sticks even though there's enough baked goods at the house to stock a bakery."

"With extra dipping sauce." She grinned and pulled out of the parking lot. "I figured you needed the comfort right now, and this is something of a celebration, too."

Shocked, I said, "How do you figure that? Did I miss the part where my misfortune is your…I don't know what since I'm not even paying you?"

Patrea snorted and spared me a look as she pointed the car down my street. "Were you at the same meeting I was? The feds are not looking at you anymore. Not seriously, anyway. This is a good thing."

"Oh, I guess that's one way to look at it. So I'm off the hook?"

"Probably. My handwriting guy is one of theirs. Or he was. Retired FBI, and the best in the country. If he says forgery, they're not going to argue the point."

While the reassurance should have made me feel better, it didn't entirely. She'd probably spent a fortune on the analysis, and I didn't have the money to pay her back. Still, I had a boatload of antiques in Catherine's lair, and Patrea could have her pick.

"Okay, then. I guess it's time to eat pizza and decorate ourselves a tree." If there was a false note of cheer in my voice, Patrea kindly overlooked it, and by the time we pulled up next to Jacy's pink monstrosity any cheer I felt had turned genuine.

"I thought we'd make a party out of it," Patrea said. "Tree trimming is more fun with a crowd, and I didn't think we needed to eat an entire pizza each."

Or she'd been so worried about me she'd felt the need to call in reinforcements. Either way, we walked into a typical Neena and Jacy squabble over whether or not the tree stood straight in the stand, and I was glad for the distraction.

"We've brought sustenance," Patrea handed me the pizza boxes and hung up her coat. Then she took them back so I could do the same, and I followed her into the parlor where we both stopped to stare.

"It's too many lights, isn't it?" Neena said. "Didn't I say that last string was too many?"

"No such thing as too many lights." Jacy grinned as she tucked the last twinkling bulb between some branches. I pretended not to see the concerned looks or subtle nods passing between the three women. "We decided to set it up in here instead of the living room since this window faces the street. Is that okay?"

"It's perfect," I said. "There's more room in here, too."

By unspoken agreement—or maybe they talked about it behind my back—the subject of Paul and the FBI stayed off the table.

Patrea and I trudged up and down the stairs, returning with a pile of bins I'd already marked as tree decorations. By the time we got back to the parlor I was so hot I considered stripping down to my underpants. Instead, I opened the front door and leaned outside, raising my arms a little to let the cold air hit me while Jacy pounced on the bins.

"Where are the lights? And tell me there's lots of garland?" she asked, opening each lid and peeking inside.

109

"You look ridiculous doing that, by the way," she laughed. "Never mind, I found it. Oh, my."

Just as with everything Catherine-related, the former owner of my house had managed to accumulate dozens of lengths of garland in varying holiday shades. I suspected we could decorate a tree for every room of the house, and still have enough to line the stair banister, the fireplace mantle, and anything else that lent itself to being draped.

"Well," Jacy said, assessing the situation. "We could go traditional red, green, silver, and gold, or we could take a page from that couple on Elm Street with the pink and purple lights I liked so much."

Neena peered into the bin and replied, "I don't know. That one was pretty, but you think Christmas tree and you immediately picture the classic red and green."

"I could go either way," I said, shooting a look at Patrea. "What's your vote?"

"I say buck tradition, let's do something pretty and girly."

With that, we were at a tie, but the girly contingency won out when Jacy mentioned—in more of a whine than she would have admitted—that since she was eating for two, she ought to get two votes.

While the lights and garland went up, the rest of us dug through more bins for coordinating decorations. "These are cute," Patrea commented, holding up a box of miniature wreaths made out of brown beads with wooden moose heads where the bows might go. She pulled one out and ran her fingers over the irregularly-shaped beads. "What are these? They're light like wood, but they look like stones."

Recognizing the handiwork of one Bess Tate, I giggled, which drew Jacy and Neena's attention. We all exchanged conspiratorial looks and burst out laughing.

"What?" Patrea asked, her fingers still clutching the ornament. "What?"

"Nothing, it's just that you're holding one of Mooselick River's most controversial exports: beads made out of petrified moose droppings."

She dropped the wreath like it was a red-hot poker, and pierced each of us with a glare. "You're telling me there's someone in this town who goes into the woods, collects moose crap, and then rolls it into little balls and waits for it to harden?"

"Well, not quite. The droppings come in little balls already. Big piles of little balls that get dried and varnished and made into wreaths and jewelry.

"You're kidding. Jewelry? You know, this is why I live in the city. Where people are normal." She went into the kitchen, washed her hands thoroughly, and then came back with a tray of decorated sugar cookies.

By the end of the night, the tree having been decorated in shades of pink and purple, and with a couple glasses of merlot in her system, Patrea managed finally managed to find the funny when it came to the wreaths. However, we did adhere to her wishes, and dumped the box of moose poop ornaments in the garbage.

I hoped Catherine wouldn't mind, and then decided if she did, that was just too bad.

# CHAPTER 16

Patrea approached Cappy's Tavern much like one might a snake: with extreme caution and trepidation. If she'd had any idea Chris Evergreen frequented the place, I'd probably have to drag her inside.

"Place looks busy," she said. "We probably won't get a table. I'm good with pizza and a movie."

"We'll get a table." It was busy for a Wednesday, but with the holidays, people were out and about. Besides, Jacy and Neena were already inside and Jacy had texted me to say Darcy Campbell was sitting a few tables over. This would be my best chance to get her side of the grocery store showdown with Amber.

"I'm sure it's nothing like what you're used to, but the food's pretty good, and most of the bands don't suck. Consider it part of your down-home Christmas experience or don't, but we're going in."

"Pretty good? Define pretty good food."

An icy wind whistled through the parking lot, pushing against our backs. It was too cold to stand and argue. "Pretty good means they have seven varieties of chicken wings, can turn out a platter of spaghetti and meatballs that would make an Italian sing for his supper, and the beer battered fish and chips are pure sin. Batter's made with a local brew and they cook the fries in duck fat. Ask for the Parmesan sprinkled, and I'm telling you, it's an experience. Now, can we go inside before my knees freeze together?"

"Duck fat fries? Okay, sold."

Finally, she got her feet moving and we stepped into the heat and noise. The band wouldn't fire up for another half hour or so, which should give us time to order and figure out a plan of attack for getting a word with Darcy. The best I'd come up with so far was to watch and follow her if she went into the ladies' room.

While I got dressed for the evening out, I'd asked Amber about the fight. She'd vibrated and poofed. An activity that in my past experience with ghosts meant she had strong feelings about what had happened or the incident had something to do with her death. Since she hadn't returned, I'd have to try and pry that information out of Darcy.

Shouldn't be too hard since we were virtual strangers, right?

To keep her from bolting, I threaded my arm through Patrea's and guided her toward our regular table on the end of a raised platform that ran around the back side of the bar. From the elevated vantage point, we could see the dance floor, the stage, and most of the other tables. These were the best seats in the house for people watching.

"What's the haps?" I slid into the seat next to Jacy while Patrea took the one on my other side. Light from a fake candle with a flickering bulb sitting atop a silk poinsettia flower pooled in the center of the table. Above our heads, the white twinkle lights that normally festooned the spokes of the wagon wheel chandelier had been switched out for colored ones twined through tinsel garland.

Those were the only nods to the season in sight, but since the motif had been repeated for every table, the place looked more festive than usual.

Jacy waved a virgin cocktail in the air and announced, "We're drinking to the closing on my house being delayed another two days. At this rate, we're going to be moving on New Year's Eve."

"What happened this time?"

113

"Who knows. It's the…wait, let me get this straight…it's a daisy chain of crazy. The people selling the house to the people we're buying ours from had to delay because their lawyer's wife had a baby. Now we all get to wait. I'm not a fan of lawyers at the moment."

Patrea stiffened, and tender-hearted as she was, Jacy caught the motion. "That came out wrong. I didn't mean all lawyers, just the ones handling this sale. I've been packed and ready since the last "firm" date."

"That's because you're nesting," Neena tipped her wine glass in Jacy's direction. "It's all going to work out; you'll be in before Christmas. I have a good feeling."

"Pfft," Jacy grinned. "You're just feeling good is all."

"I am not, this is only my first glass of wine. I won't be feeling good until my third. We ordered a wings sampler for the table, should be here anytime."

"A sampler for you guys, and a bowl of tomato soup for me. Peanut has decided meat is not for us this week."

Miranda Perkins showed up with the soup and sampler and took the rest of our drink order while I scanned the place looking for Darcy Campbell. I spotted her at a table with her husband, or at least I assumed it was him since I could only see the back of the man's head.

"There's Darcy." Jacy noticed the direction I was looking. "She doesn't look good. Attack of conscience over fighting with Amber, I bet."

No, more like an attack of the willies because Amber sat in the next seat and kept poking her arm through Darcy's body. "Listen, I have to visit the ladies, order me the fish and chips when Miranda comes back, okay? And save me a couple of wings." I grabbed my purse and hustled across the bar before anyone could follow.

As I passed by the Campbell table, I let my purse strap dangle and catch the back of the chair Amber hovered over. When the chair yanked at the strap, I feigned a stumble and turned to face the seated couple.

114

"I'm sorry, I'm having a clumsy moment." Letting my eyes go wide, I looked at Darcy's husband. "You're Nelson, right? We were in school together. Everly Dupree. I'm awful sorry about the tragic loss of your cousin." Whose face I stared into as I offered my sympathies. Amber took the hint and let Darcy alone.

"I remember you." From his neutral tone, I couldn't tell if that was a good thing or a bad thing. Or if maybe I should have avoided such a painful subject. "Thanks."

He said no more, and after a few seconds of awkward silence, I gave Amber a subtle nod and walked away. She followed me to the bathroom where I dallied around with washing my hands until we had a moment alone. "I don't care what beef you had with Darcy, what you were doing is not cool. You have no idea how creepy it feels."

"She deserved it," was all Amber managed before the door opened again. Darcy walked in and burst into tears. Because it's what you do, I patted her on the back and said something along the lines of, "There, there." The next thing I knew, she'd launched herself into my arms and was sobbing on my shoulder. The smell of barley and hops practically oozed from her pores. Darcy had had a few more than a few too many.

"What am I going to do? He hates me now, and that witch had to go and get herself killed so I can't make things right. How am I supposed to tell her I'm sorry now?"

My eyes met Amber's and I said the only thing I could say under the circumstances. "Why don't you go ahead and speak your piece. I bet, wherever she is, Amber will hear and she'll forgive you." Her daggered look said she wouldn't, but Darcy didn't have to know that.

"I didn't know Nelson's grandmother promised that angel topper to Amber, and I didn't ask her to give it to me, either. Gertie's memory was going, and she gave it to me when we helped pack her place up so she could go stay with Pete."

"You and Amber got into a public fight over a Christmas ornament?"

"Yeah. Well, no. It was mostly because Amber acted like some hotshot celebrity, ordering me around and wantin' fancy cheese and stuff. I got mad, and then the topper, well, that topped the whole thing off. She acted like we'd broken into her house and stolen something from her. Said she was going to get a lawyer and sue me, so I got mad."

Darcy finally let go of me, and I noted with dismay she'd left mascara stains on my shirt.

"I probably overreacted," Amber admitted. "A little."

"Now my husband hates me and I think my marriage is over because I was the reason Amber died. She left and went to that motel because of me."

"Oh crap. Now I'm the jerk," Amber said. "Tell her...never mind, you don't do messages to family."

"Listen, Darcy. You weren't to blame for Amber's death, and deep down, your husband knows that. He's feeling guilty because he's playing the shoulda coulda woulda game. I don't know why Amber died, and I hope the police are able to figure out who killed her, but it wasn't you."

Not knowing if I'd get another chance, I took a stab at prying some information out of Darcy. "Do you know if she was worried about anything else while she was staying with you? Or scared of anyone?"

"Far be it from me to speak ill of the dead, but that girl didn't have the sense to be scared." Darcy shivered again as, looking annoyed, Amber drilled a finger through her upper arm.

"Sorry, she gets on my last nerve." Darcy couldn't hear the apology, but if she had, she'd have known it wasn't sincere.

"All she talked about was you. She was going to nail you to the wall, or so she said. I'm sorry, but I guess there's no harm in telling you now. You didn't kill her, did you?" Darcy tipped her head back to look at me, and almost overbalanced herself.

"No, I didn't kill her," I sighed. "If I was going to kill anyone it would be my ex."

"Only other thing I remember is Amber was supposed to talk to some woman who said she had inside information that would prove you sub…sub," Darcy squinted and tried to come up with the word she wanted to say. "Did something wrong."

"Do you have a name?"

"She didn't say." When she caught sight of herself in the mirror, Darcy forgot all about me while she pulled a tube of lipstick out of her bag and smeared it over half of her face. I finally had to step in and help.

"There, I think you're almost presentable again. You should probably go back to your table before your husband thinks you've run out the back."

"He won't hardly even look at me."

"He will, you just need to go back out there and talk to him. Tell him you love him, and that you know he's feeling bad because he didn't protect his cousin. Tell him you feel bad, too, and that you're sorry for fighting with her. I'm sure she'd apologize if she could. Then you think about the good times you had before the fight, and you remind him of how much they meant to each other. He'll come around. You just need to love on him until he does."

Darcy swiped her arm across her nose before I could get her something better to use. "Love on him. I can do that. Thanks." Wobbling only a little, she left Amber and me behind.

"Were you really going to sue Darcy over a Christmas tree topper?"

Amber's face pinked. "Maybe. And maybe that lawyer told me I was an idiot."

"Well, if he did, he was right. What was the angel made out of? Gold?"

"Not exactly," Amber shrugged. "Cardboard and cotton fluff mostly. It's just that she brought back memories and I wanted her."

With the drama over, I detoured around Darcy and her husband on my way back to the table, but I couldn't help taking a peek at them once I sat back down. They were holding hands across the table, and when she felt my gaze upon her, Darcy looked up at me and gave a watery smile.

"I guess we can cross Darcy off our suspect list," I said as I chose one of the house special wings. "She and Amber were fighting over something silly." I recounted the events of my bathroom encounter.

"Okay," Patrea tossed her wing bones on the pile. "I give up. What's the secret ingredient? I taste salt and something a little acidic, but there's another flavor I can't quite place."

Grinning, Neena put her out of her misery. "It's dill. They soak the wings overnight in pickle brine to make them tender."

"Well, it works. They're perfection. Practically fall off the bone." Patrea tipped up her beer, took a long swallow, then just about choked. When her eyes went wide, I swiveled to see why, and caught the swagger on Chris Evergreen walking through the door.

Oh, this was going to be fun.

I watched Patrea watch him as he took a raised two-top near the dance floor. Her breath quickened, then she dragged her gaze away and focused on the plate Miranda put in front of her. "If this tastes half as good as it looks, I'm going to have to admit to being a fan of Mooselick River cuisine."

"We don't boast the fanciest atmosphere, but the guy who runs the kitchen moved here from New York a couple of years back." I reached for the malt vinegar to douse a few of my fries.

Nipping one off Patrea's plate, Jacy popped it in her mouth and sighed. "The guy quit his job at a five-star restaurant to move to the boonies and make us all worship his ability to turn potatoes and duck fat into morsels of heaven."

"Does that happen a lot?" Patrea asked with interest.

"People come for a visit and get hooked on the slower pace?"

"Why?" Neena wanted to know. "Have you succumbed to the wiles of small-town living?"

Patrea shrugged. "It doesn't suck. Why did you stay on after your husband passed?"

"Can't say I'm a huge fan of the winters, or the fact his mother lives close enough to spit on my front step, but I feel at home here and I couldn't see any reason to leave."

Jacy leaned over to give Neena a shoulder nudge. "I'm glad you stayed." It could have been baby hormones, or just genuine emotion, but she teared up a little. "You're helping me live out my dream."

"Mine, too. I have my own gallery space, and if Everly and her posse of old ladies have their way, we'll all be rolling in tourist money next summer."

I blew on a bite of flaky, white fish to cool it down some. "Martha has half a dozen schemes in the works already. She's determined to bring Mooselick River back to its former heyday or die trying. Her words, not mine."

"She's been badgering Mabel," having ordered a salad to appease Peanut's food sensibilities, Jacy eyed the crispy perfection of my battered haddock nuggets, "to do something, and I quote, 'to make the diner look more appealing to tourists'. You can imagine Mabel's response." Unable to quell the craving, she reached across and swiped some fish off my plate.

"Martha's a spry old bird, but probably not nimble enough to jump up her own ass." Neena's dry response pulled a rare laugh out of Patrea. Out of the corner of my eye, I saw Chris Evergreen's head swivel in our direction. And I almost felt the heat when his attention locked on her. Not cut out for romance, was she? We'd see about that.

119

# CHAPTER 17

When the band kicked into its first number, Neena dragged Jacy off to the dance floor where, even pregnant, she moved with her usual grace.

"Do you have any idea how lucky you are?" I didn't think it was a couple of beers talking when Patrea pitched her voice to be heard above the music. "Those two are absolute gold. Friends you can count on no matter what."

"I do, and they are. You know you're one of us now, right?"

I grinned at the half-shocked, half-pleased look on her face. "It's not like you have to kill a chicken at midnight and dance naked under the full moon to be accepted into the group. Jacy only steals fries from friends, you know."

Before things turned too emotional, I decided to follow Jacy's lead and drag Patrea out to dance. Chris had the same idea, and beat me to it. He appeared like a ghost next to us, and when she looked up at him, she blushed. That was one for the books.

"May I have the honor?" He held out his hand and, as though she'd fallen under a spell, Patrea took it. She spared a quick glance back as he led her away. I couldn't tell if what I saw was panic or wonder on her face. Being the friend I am, I joined Jacy and Neena, who had a front row seat for the show.

And what a show it was.

"Did you know he could dance like that?" The man looked like a lumberjack but danced like a stripper, and Patrea matched him move for move.

"I'm not sure I can keep watching. It's not decent." Neena's eyes flashed with humor, and I noticed she didn't look away. Half the eyes in the place seemed riveted. "Whoa, I feel a hot flash coming on."

Grinning a mile wide, Jacy predicted some husbands and boyfriends of the women watching were going to get lucky later, and by the gleam in her eye, I figured Brian would be one of them.

The next song was a slow one, so the three of us went back to our table to watch the dance of the raging hormones. I held back a smile when Amber popped in next to me and said, "He didn't dance with me like that."

When Miranda stopped by to see if we wanted another round of drinks, she leaned in and fanned herself with a coaster. "Looks like those two ought to get a room."

To stay under the legal limit, I ordered a soft drink and then asked, "Does he do this kind of thing often?" If Chris was the type to pick up a new woman every night, I figured I could find a way to warn Patrea.

"Chris likes to get his groove on. He was a dancer on Broadway until his father took sick and he came back to run the farm." Lacy watched him a moment longer, "But I ain't never seen him dance with anyone like that, if that's what you're asking. Gives a girl the tingles. Too bad, though, because it looks like your friend there has a shot at taking that piece of prime meat off the market."

The way he wrapped himself around her while they swayed to a slow song, I thought Miranda might be right.

"Time to change the subject." I filled Jacy and Neena in on the latest news from the Hastings debacle.

"I'm sorry you had to talk to the FBI. That's terrifying." Jacy reached across the table to press my hand gently.

"Patrea was right there, and she deflected their attention off of me. I don't think I'm their prime suspect anymore, but I keep wondering if any of this is connected to Amber's death.

The agents didn't bring it up, but don't you think the timing is suspicious?"

"Is it, though?" Neena said thoughtfully. "She was here to talk to you, but wasn't she killed before you knew about the interview she'd done with Paul? There could be a connection."

Sure there was. "Me, you mean."

"Do you think Paul could have killed her?" I'd been contemplating that question for some time, so when Jacy asked it, I had a ready answer.

"No, I don't. But then, I didn't think he was a liar, a cheat, or a thief, either, so I could be wrong."

Jacy picked up the salt shaker that was still on the table from our meal, and shook a white blizzard into her Pepsi. When we cringed, she shrugged. "I'm gestating and the baby wants what it wants."

"Nasty," was all Neena said, but it took a moment to remember what we'd been talking about.

"It all comes down to motive and I can't see what motive Paul would have had for killing Amber. As far as he knew, she'd given him a prime chance to cast shade on me—publicly. Once his face was splashed all over the news, no one would believe me if I said the sky was blue. He can be very convincing when he wants to be." I knew that better than anyone.

"Still, she was murdered here, in Mooselick River, so that's got to play a part, right?"

This was a point I'd considered. "Could be. She does have family ties to the area, so it could have been personal. Or it could have been work related. There were other reporters in town trying to get an interview with me. Maybe she stepped on someone's toes. Then, there was the cameraman she was sleeping with."

"Wait," Jacy's mouth rounded in surprise. "How did you find that out?"

"Well, we found something of hers in his room when we cleaned up the motel." I backtracked quickly. Jacy knew about

122

my past hauntings, but Neena didn't, so I'd have to keep my source for the information under wraps. "I put two and two together. Plus, I heard him talking on this phone the night of the lighting contest, and the way he talked about her was more personal than if they were just coworkers."

Something—or more accurately, someone—caught my eye at the bar. "Speak of the devil. That's the guy, right over there. His name is Lance." I pointed, and both their heads swiveled in that direction.

"You mean that lump of a man hunched over the bar?" Jacy asked.

I nodded. "That would be the one. I'll be right back," I said and hopped off my stool.

Picking my way through the crowd, I made it to the bar just in time to realize I wouldn't be getting any pertinent information out of Lance after all. His head rested on his hands, and though I couldn't hear him over the din I could tell he was snoring by the way the drool dripping from his mouth bubbled with each exhale.

"Friend of yours?" Milo Lynch, the bartender, asked while shooting a disdainful look in Lance's direction.

"No," I said with a shake of my head, "but I've seen him around." I didn't mention he'd been skulking around my front porch with the rest of the news crews. "He's a cameraman for the channel five news."

Milo looked like he'd just had an epiphany and snapped his fingers. "That's who he was talking about. The dead reporter, Amber something-or-other. Sleet, maybe."

"Hale. Amber Hale," I corrected automatically, the hairs on the back of my neck standing at attention. "What did he say about her?"

With a shrug, Milo began mixing another drink and explained, "He's just been moaning her name for the last forty-five minutes, and he mumbled something about something being 'her fault'. Sounded like he had a thing for her, so I assumed he was just another victim of a pre-holiday

123

dumping. You'd be surprised by how far some people would go to avoid having to buy another Christmas gift."

And that, folks, is just another of the many reasons I have no interest in dating.

"Does he have a lift back to the Bide-A-Way?" I asked. "That's where he's been staying."

Milo nodded and passed a cup of whipped cream-topped eggnog to a customer at the other end of the bar. "Already called him a cab," he shouted in my direction.

Since he seemed to have it covered, and the snoring had grown loud enough for me to hear it, I cast one more look at the pathetic looking Lance, and returned to my friends.

"Any luck?" Jacy asked, but without any real interest. She couldn't tear her eyes away from something on the dance floor.

I didn't bother answering and instead turned to watch with fascination as Chris's lips lowered, almost in slow motion, to meet Patrea's. The music swelled at just the right moment, making me wonder if, along with Amber's ghost, a Christmas angel had decided to pay a visit to Mooselick River.

"Well, I'll be…" I said, just as Neena and Jacy broke into applause loud enough to turn the couple's heads in our direction.

Patrea blushed, but the sparkle in her eye didn't dim. She approached the table with Chris's arm wrapped securely around her waist, and whispered in my ear, "I think I'm about to get my Hallmark moment. Don't wait up." With a wink at Jacy and Neena, she followed behind Chris and the pair disappeared into the crowd.

Neena shivered and raised her glass, "Here's to Patrea, and a mind-blowing night of torrid lust!"

"Hear, hear!" we clinked glasses and toasted our new friend.

Now it was Jacy's eyes that were sparkling. "I suspect there's more than lust there; I smelled the distinct scent of love in the air."

Maybe it was just the holiday spirit, or maybe it was the fact that I'd seen the sparks fly from the moment Chris laid eyes on Patrea, but somehow, I thought Jacy might be right.

# CHAPTER 18

"Here you go, girl."

Just as I leaned down to put Molly's dish on the floor, a knock on the door made me jump and spill kibble everywhere. Molly's tail whirled as she chased down the nuggets, which I tried to avoid as I worked up a mock lecture for Patrea since she'd stayed out all night.

The words died on my tongue when I saw Ernie standing on my porch.

"What can I do for you?" The look on his face was enough to tell me I wouldn't like the answer.

"I need to ask you some questions."

What else was new?

"Come on in, then."

Ernie hesitated. "Official questions."

"Are there any other kind?" I frowned up at him. "Look, I'm not going to run out the back door and wallow through snow drifts to go on the lam. Come inside and ask me anything you want, but you'd better let me have my coffee first or I can't promise you my answers will be coherent."

Sighing, Ernie relented and followed me to the kitchen.

"I take it you haven't seen the local news this morning." He settled into a chair at the table and nodded when I held up a large mug as an offer of caffeinated sustenance.

"Nope. Want some eggs to go with that?" Whatever had happened, I'd handle it better on a full stomach.

Leaning back hard enough to make the chair creak, Ernie commented. "You could at least act like you're intimidated.

Most people are when I show up on their doorstep during the course of a murder investigation."

Still, he held up two fingers when I pulled out the carton of eggs and asked for toast.

"I figure if you thought I'd killed anyone, you'd have slapped the cuffs on me already." I poured coffee into both cups and went back to stirring the eggs as they cooked, "But I'm dying to hear what brought you to my door so early."

"Does the name Reva McKinnon mean anything to you?"

I took a moment to think and cook. When the eggs were done and my thoughts were in order, I plunked a plate in front of him and turned back for silverware. "It does. Has something happened to her?" One could only hope.

Pausing to douse his eggs with a hail of salt and pepper, Ernie kept me on tenterhooks until he finally answered. "No, not exactly. You really should have watched the news this morning."

"Maybe," I said as forked up a bite that I was sure tasted like cardboard. "You could tell me what's going on because I've clearly missed something."

When he goes into full cop mode, Ernie doesn't miss much, but since I had nothing to hide, I looked him straight in the eyes while I waited for an explanation.

"Miss McKinnon made some serious allegations about you in an interview on the channel five news, so now I have to ask. What was your relationship with Amber Hale and where were you when she was killed?"

I couldn't help it, I rolled my eyes so hard they hurt. "Are you serious?"

"As a heart attack."

"We have gone over all of this before." I pointed a piece of toast at him. "Until she showed up here, I'd never met the woman, and to the best of my recollection the only thing I ever said to her was that I had nothing to say to her." While she was living, anyhow.

127

"You did tell me to go away, but that was through the door." Helpful as always, Amber confirmed, and to my credit, I didn't even jump when she appeared over Ernie's left shoulder.

His face a stony mask, Ernie said, "Miss McKinnon's story suggests otherwise."

"Does it, now?" I propped my elbows on the table and dropped my chin into cupped hands. "I'd just love to hear what Reva had to say on the subject of a non-conversation she wasn't even present to witness. Do enlighten me, won't you?"

In his most dry tone and using spare language, Ernie painted an ugly and almost entirely fictitious picture of my recent encounter with Reva, one I hoped no one who knew me would believe. Except that here was Ernie, sitting at my kitchen table with that look on his face.

By the time he finished, I wasn't sure whether to laugh or cry.

"I'll give her points for having a vivid imagination, but I notice she didn't mention she was sleeping with my husband while we were married. Or that she accused me of some ridiculous attempt to win Paul back, and when I called her on it, assaulted me on my front porch." Involuntarily, my hand lifted to touch the cheek she'd reddened. "Molly only went after her because she slapped me."

I might have to eat crow in front of Patrea, but her idea of setting up a video security system for the house was sounding better all the time.

Ernie didn't seem to find this new information compelling. "Most people have the common sense to call the police in situations like you experienced. Funny, I don't remember getting a call from you."

"It was a slap in the face, not a knock-down-drag-out fight. Molly heard the commotion, and came to my rescue. Reva lost her footing and fell, I pulled the dog back, told Reva to leave and she did. That's the gist of it. If Reva turned up dead, I could see you knocking on my door and asking questions. But Amber? I had no motive and there's no evidence against me."

"Your name was on the order for the string of lights that was used to kill Amber Hale." The blandly offered statement turned my blood to ice.

"It was, and if you saw that, you noticed the order was placed on the third of November. When did Amber interview Paul?"

"December seventh," she said helpfully.

"And didn't you state that Amber Hale had been harassing you for an interview?"

"I don't think I used the word harassing, but she was persistent. She wasn't the only one looking for a sound bite, though. Are any other reporters dead?"

"And isn't it a fact that the station pulled an interview with your ex-husband out of their line-up solely on the basis of Amber Hale's death? And didn't that give you time to offer a statement of your own that aired instead?"

At about that time, my body went numb. None of this was evidence, but none of it made me look good, either. "Believe it or not, I didn't know anything about Paul's interview until after Amber was killed."

"Then you won't mind telling me your source for that information."

That, my friend, is how I ended up between the rock and the hard place.

"I...uh," I stammered and wished hard for Patrea to show up and save my butt, but of course, she was off canoodling with her Christmas toy. "It's complicated, but I can assure you I didn't strangle Amber in the hopes her death would kill a story I didn't even know she'd done. Even you can see there's a lack of logic in that theory."

Ernie took offense to my tone. In retrospect, I can see why.

"You don't seriously think I killed Amber, do you?"

Ernie rose to put his dishes in the sink. "Under the right circumstances, everyone has the capacity to commit murder."

"That's not an answer."

Heaving a sigh, he put me out of my misery. "No, I'm not looking at you for the murder of Amber Hale. None of the evidence points to you. It takes a lot of determination to strangle someone. No offense, but I can't see you having the strength to pull it off, but I had to follow up on the allegations made."

"None taken," I rose to fill his coffee cup, and because a little fat and sugar are always good for calming the nerves, offered him one of Patrea's pastries.

"He's an idiot. You could totally kill someone if you wanted to." Amber threw a vote of confidence my way. Misplaced and unwelcome as it might be.

"Have you talked to Darcy Campbell?" I'd ruled her out based on a drunken conversation, but he might have talked to her when she was sober.

Ernie stuffed half a coffee bar in his mouth, and blew out a few crumbs when he spoke. "Not hardly. If anyone would have turned up dead because of that dust up, it would have been Darcy, not Amber."

Selecting a second coffee bar, Ernie rose to leave. "McKinnon's interview got the feds stirred up again. There might be nothing come of it, but I thought you should know they're asking questions."

"Thanks for the heads up." Tipping me off had to break some professional courtesy rule, and I appreciated the warning.

At the door, he hesitated, "You're a constant annoyance to me, but this is my town and I'm sworn to protect and serve the people here. Watch your back, Everly, or Reva McKinnon's likely to stick a knife in it."

"Isn't he dramatic?" Amber repeated Ernie's final statement, imitated his tone. "You sure you don't want to take that trip to Paris? It might be our last chance before Reva takes you down."

The doorbell rang just as Ernie put his hand on the knob. Without thinking, he opened the door to Mia James and a barrage of irrelevant questions about my sex life with Paul.

For the rest of the day, with Ernie in the foreground, my white face and bemused expression would be featured as the blurb to beckon people to see more on the five o'clock news. So yeah, I had that going for me.

Out of reflex, Ernie slammed the door in her face. "Quite the interesting life you lead," he said in his driest tone.

"Are you kidding me with those questions?" Amber practically screeched in my ear. "What is that idiot thinking?"

"I have no idea." I muttered, but I didn't really care about Amber's feelings at the moment, though at least she was a distraction from the cesspool that was turning out to be my life.

Pacing, or rather floating back and forth, Amber ranted. "They better not be planning to give that anchor job to Mia James. Mia Freaking James. She's as vacant as a condemned hotel."

Amber's fury prickled along my skin and lifted the hairs on the back of my neck. If she ever learned she could affect the physical world, Mia had better hope Amber didn't know where she lived.

When the doorbell rang again, Ernie practically yanked the door off its hinges and roared for Mia to get the hell off my front porch. The look on her face was priceless. At least Amber thought so. She laughed herself silly, then fizzled away.

"If there wasn't a chance you'd toss me in jail for it, I'd kiss you right now." Call me petty, but I found great satisfaction when the tips of his ears burned red and Ernie bulled his way past Mia, who now stood a few steps back from the porch.

He didn't say anything to her or acknowledge her furious stare, but he did stop and talk to Lance Colby—who, to my surprise, looked no worse for the wear despite his drunken stupor the evening before—when the cameraman stepped into Ernie's path. I couldn't hear what was said, but Ernie's posture stiffened, and Lance's hands curled into fists. Distracted enough to forget all about me, Mia watched Lance closely, her brow furrowed and her lips pressed into a firm line.

Ernie spared one look back at her, and based on what happened next, told Lance to get Mia off my property.

Taking advantage of the moment of inattentiveness, I stepped back inside and closed the door.

It would have been petty to let Molly loose on the front porch, and she was just as likely to make new friends as defend her territory. So, I hunkered down on the hallway stairs and contemplated the exact point where I lost control of my life. That there were so many possible options it was depressing.

By the time Neena walked through the door without knocking, I'd decided to find the whole thing amusing.

"Hey, Neena. Welcome to chaos, want a cookie? I've got a bunch of stuff in the kitchen. Is Mia still out there? We could send her out a plate."

"Better send out several, then, because there's a crowd out there now." Neena hugged me. "I had to fight my way in."

Apparently, the lilt in my tone gave Neena cause for concern. "I saw all of this," she circled a hand in vaguely the direction of my driveway, "on my way to the shop, so I thought I'd better check on you."

"Oh, it's nothing really. I'm under suspicion for murder because Reva gave an interview filled with lies. I'm not exactly sure what she said, but I got the news from Ernie Polk when he showed up to ask me, for approximately the hundredth tie, where I was when Amber was killed."

Thunder rolled, and lightning crashed. Not literally, but I got that same feeling of anticipation that comes just before a storm when Neena's gaze raked over me. "He can't be serious. Where's Patrea? She'll handle Ernie."

"She didn't come home last night."

"Okay, now I'm sorry I have to go to work. I'd love to be here when she shows up." Neena hugged me and headed for the door. "Get all the juicy details and call me if you need anything."

I smiled and rose to grab a coat, clip on Molly's leash, and follow Neena out onto the porch. "Tell Jacy I'm okay. This is just a blip." I meant it, too. Ernie didn't scare me, but I noticed his outburst had cleared the porch, and Mia must have passed the word because only she and Lance remained on the property. The rest of the reporters paced around on the sidewalk in an attempt to stay warm.

Mia and Lance stood quite close together, talking low enough I couldn't hear what they were saying, but the way she looked at him, I didn't need to. Cats look at mice just that way. Amber's body was barely cold, and even if she insisted she'd only been having fun with Lance, Mia hadn't waited long before moving on him.

With his back turned toward me, I couldn't tell if she was making inroads or not, but he did have his hands shoved in his pockets and was leaning slightly away from her, so I thought maybe not.

Wherever Amber had faded off to, I hope she'd stay there for a while.

Icy wind needled right through my clothes to bite into flesh. Molly went stiff-legged at the end of her lead, fur standing on end along her spine, and a low growl rumbling in her throat.

"It's the attack dog." Mia squealed in terror and jumped at Lance to wrap her legs around his waist and cling. He staggered and nearly fell.

"Don't let it bite my face. I'll be scarred for life."

133

Out of morbid curiosity, I considered dropping Molly's leash to see if Mia could shimmy her way up to Lance's shoulders. He held up under the assault, but snapped out an order for her to get hold of herself and followed it up with, "Don't be an idiot."

Eyes still locked on Molly, Mia ignored the idiot comment, uncurled herself, and put booted feet back on the ground. "Do you deny your dog attacked Reva McKinnon without provocation?"

It was probably useless to defend my dog, but I did it anyway. "I suppose that depends on what you consider provocation. Does my being assaulted on my own porch count? Or did Reva leave out the part where she hit me?"

Mia frowned and took a couple of seconds to process the new information.

"No, I see she gave you her version of events and it never occurred to you to ask for mine before you aired the footage."

Sensing an opening, Mia's expression turned crafty. "We're here now, let's hear your side of the story. Lance, are you ready to roll?"

I held up a hand to stop him before he could get hold of his camera and point it toward me. "Don't bother."

With Molly walking sedately at my side, I approached the first reporter that wasn't Mia. "You." I pointed at random. "Come back this afternoon, and we'll talk. The rest of you," I raised my voice to just under a shout, "should go find a story more interesting than airing my dirty laundry. It's Christmas— surely there's something more uplifting to talk about."

Score one for Everly, I thought, then turned to see Lance angle his camera at Mia who announced, "Given that new facts have come to light, local police questioned Everly Dupree in connection with the death of our very own Amber Hale. Stay tuned for more breaking news as the situation progresses."

134

# CHAPTER 19

*You'd better get back here before I do something else stupid.*

I sent an SOS text to Patrea. Being under siege made me cranky. Being under siege three days before Christmas when I was supposed to help drop off gift baskets turned up the heat until cranky threatened to boil over.

To burn off the mad, I tore apart the kitchen for a session of deep cleaning.

"You want me to go out and poke Mia a few times?" Amber faded in.

"Tempting, but no." Her voice sounded muffled since I was half inside one of the lower cabinets wiping out the deepest corners. "Tell me about her, and leave out the hyperbole."

"Not much to tell. She's ambitious but lacks the instincts for what makes a good story, so she asks ridiculous questions. I'm not sure she can tell the difference between news and scandal."

I scuffled back on my hands and knees and started putting things back on the shelves. "Probably why she was asking questions about my sex life this morning like that had anything to do with Amber's death or the stupid allegations Reva made."

"That boring, huh?"

My face flamed. "By your standards? Yeah, I'm sure it was."

"Are you a prude or was Paul just not very inventive?" Amber wrinkled her nose.

"Stay on topic." I closed the cabinet door, and tossed the dirty cloth into the sink.

Amber grinned. "You're the one who brought up your sex life, I was merely establishing the context of the discussion."

If I'd had the dirty cloth still in my hand, I might have thrown it through her at that point. Instead, I pointed out, "Seems like you and Mia have one thing in common: an inappropriate level of interest in my personal life."

"It's not like I have anything else to do. You're the only person who can talk to me."

I seized on the chance she presented. "Then it's in your best interest to help me solve your murder so you can move on to wherever it is you're supposed to go. I'm sure there will be plenty of people to talk to on the other side of the light."

She probably shouldn't quote me on that, though, given my lack of actual experience.

"Tell me everything you remember about the days before you died."

I should have specified I didn't need the salacious details of her tryst with Lance, but I suspect Amber was only trying to get a reaction out of me. Partway through the recounting, when Molly dropped her tennis ball at my feet for the third time, I hadn't learned anything useful in finding Amber's killer and I had a serious case of TMI.

Grabbing Molly's leash and an old, warped tennis racket, I prepared to run the gauntlet. It wasn't Molly's fault I couldn't turn around anymore without a news team to report on my progress, and she needed more exercise than a romp in the backyard could provide. On weekdays, because it was empty then, we'd been using the Methodist church parking lot for a game of fetch.

"I'm taking the dog out for some play time. We'll have to finish this later." Secretly, I hoped Amber would find

136

something else to occupy her time. Nothing she'd told me had been helpful, and I didn't think it was because she was holding out. She had no idea why she was dead or who had a motive to kill her.

The street in front of my house held not a single car with station numbers splashed across the sides.

"Guess they got bored with waiting around. No great loss, huh Molly girl? Let's go play ball."

The phrase play ball is like Molly's on and off switch. As soon as she hears it, she's ready to go. Breath pluming white in the chilled air, I tucked my collar up around my face and pulled my hat down low. Even if Mia drove by, she wouldn't recognize me with only my nose showing.

A pickup truck with Evergreen Farms written on the door turned into the drive just ahead of us. My wayward guest had returned.

"Walk of shame." Grinning, Amber hovered on the porch. I kept my eyes averted as I passed by the truck, and hissed at her to give Patrea some privacy.

"It's not like she can see me anyway."

"Just do the polite thing for once."

I moved wide around Amber to go inside, and when I did, she let out a whistle. "Hey, I know that guy. I danced with him at that excuse for a bar the night before I was killed." She followed me inside.

"Danced with him," I waggled my eyebrows, "Or *danced* with him?"

"Now who has their mind in the gutter? Danced. Not between the sheets, though I wouldn't have turned down the chance. The way that man can move…takes a woman's breath away."

Anyone with eyes would find it hard to argue the point, but I'd also seen the surly side of Chris. "Was there a reason it didn't happen? I mean, you're not exactly the type to hold back when it comes to putting yourself out there."

Amber opened her mouth to answer, but nothing came out. I'd seen the same thing happen before when a ghost came too close to speaking about the events leading to their death. Now, and I looked out the window to check, Patrea was all snuggled up and cozy under the arm of a possible killer.

Fan-freaking-tastic. Another awkward conversation in my future.

"What's wrong with me? I can't—" Amber's body shook with the effort to speak, and then she poofed.

"Oh sure," I said, "dump your personal junk all over me and then flit away so I have to deal with it alone. You ghosts are all alike. I don't know why I put up with you." Of course, I did. I didn't have a choice.

As the minutes passed and Patrea didn't come in, I ran through half a dozen ways to drop the bomb on her, each one sounding more outrageous than the last. I'd feel horrible about lying to her, but I didn't want to tell her about Amber. There was maybe an ounce of wiggle room between those two extremes—if I was being optimistic, and wearing rose-colored glasses.

Since I was neither, I burned off the worry by running the dust cloth over the stair banisters. I was not hanging around in the front hallway waiting for Patrea, and you can't prove I was. I also didn't jump half out of my skin when she came through the door with Chris right on her heels.

"Hey, Everly." She started toward the kitchen and then jumped when my voice came from almost directly above her.

"I'm up here. Hey Chris." Patrea looked happy—they both did. "I made coffee and we have about a dozen different kinds of baked goods in the kitchen. You must be starving after all the…um…because…it's close to noon, and--" I bit my own tongue to shut off the flow of insanity.

"I could go for a cup of coffee," Patrea put me out of my misery. "And then you can explain what stupid thing you've done."

138

"I told some guy from channel seven—or maybe it was channel two, I can't remember—anyway, I told him to come back this afternoon and I'd give him an exclusive."

All vestige of humor gone, Patrea waved the coffeepot my way, "Well, that's not going to happen. Next?"

"What makes you think there's a next?" Chris said.

"Oh, there's a next. Everly tends to bury the lede."

"That's a rude thing to say to me." I didn't put any heat behind the protest because she was probably right. "Reva was on the morning news."

Patrea called Reva a name that made Chris wince. "And what did Reva say on the morning news?"

"Well, that's the thing, I didn't see the broadcast personally. Ernie showed up here asking questions based on her allegations, so I had to take his word for it, but he made it sound pretty bad. He said she accused me of stealing the charity money, and the next thing I knew, he was asking if I killed Amber to keep Paul's interview off the air."

Patrea set my favorite mug down hard enough to slop coffee on the table. "That's some half-assed logic."

"That's what I said." I stirred creamer into my coffee, then tore off a small strip from my cinnamon roll. "Ernie took the comment as a criticism of his professional abilities, which I suppose was accurate."

"Okay, I think I'm following along here," Chris said. "You wanted to clear the air and tell your side of things, so you chose a rival station thinking you'd get a fair shake."

I muttered, "something like that."

"Hah," Patrea snorted. "You don't like Mia James, and you wanted to tweak her strings a little."

"You know your worst trait is always being right."

Chris watched the exchange with a neutral expression on his face, but I got the sense if I'd put any heat behind the mild criticism, he'd have jumped in to defend Patrea. I liked that about him even if I thought he might be a suspect in Amber's death.

"Chris, there's something I need to ask you about the night before Amber died."

"What—" Patrea started to ask but I held up a hand to stop her, and to my surprise, she went silent.

"I have it on good authority that you were with Amber at Crabby's that night." I'd have felt less like a jerk for kicking puppies than I did for poking a pin through Patrea's bubble of happiness.

As I watched his face for signs of guilt, it occurred to me that if he'd killed one woman, he might not find it a hardship to kill two more.

"Define with," was all he said.

"You were seen dancing with her."

"I dance with a lot of people." He neither confirmed nor denied the accusation, and the tension around the table cranked up a notch. "No crime in dancing."

If I hadn't spent so much time with her lately, I wouldn't have noticed the shade of pale that settled over Patrea's skin. Or that her jaw had gone tight with strain.

At least she was easier to read, because Chris could rival a sphinx when it came to blanking out any clue to his thoughts. The beard didn't help, either. Or the fact that he didn't offer up any further information.

If you look up awkward in the dictionary, I'm pretty sure you'll find a picture of the three of us sitting at my kitchen table trying hard not to look at each other. That went on for a couple of minutes, and then Chris stood to leave.

Patrea let him go without saying a word. He looked back at her once, and though it looked like it cost her, she maintained a neutral mask that forced him to do the same.

An even more awkward silence sat between us until Patrea broke it matter-of-factly. "Well, that's that, I guess. It was fun while it lasted."

"I'm sorry. I didn't know he'd break up with you like that."

"It was a one-night thing, nothing more." She could talk like it didn't matter, but I saw her fingers tremble when Patrea stood and reached for my plate with the half-eaten roll still sitting forlornly in the middle. "Didn't I tell you I'm not cut out for romance? No harm, no foul."

"Don't trivialize this." Standing, I took the plates from her and put them in the sink. "I wrecked something good that was happening for you, and I'm sorry."

"What if he's a killer? Would you still be sorry then? You might have just saved my life."

"Do you think he is?"

"No, but right now, it's easier if I convince myself he could be." It was the closest she'd come to admitting vulnerability.

Still, she went into the front room and peeked out past the branches of the Christmas tree to make sure he'd gone. If there was anything I could do to patch up my gaffe, I vowed to try. After all, didn't most holiday romance movies have a misunderstanding at the beginning of the third act? Maybe this was hers and Patrea could still get a happy ending.

# CHAPTER 20

"What's next on the holiday agenda?" We'd cleaned up the kitchen, but since I'd alrcady been there and done that, there wasn't enough work to burn off Patrea's bad mood. "We haven't made popcorn strings, or sung carols yet. Are you sure there's not a pageant of some sort running? I feel the need for festivities."

"It's Saturday, right?" The days had begun to run together. "There's a group of ladies in town who do up some holiday boxes every year. They start collecting things right after Thanksgiving, and then the Saturday before Christmas, they deliver. I'm sure they could some extra help with that this year."

There would be more boxes than ever because I'd helped them ramp up their efforts and this year, we'd collected toys and other items along with food, so I knew Martha would welcome the help.

"Playing Santa definitely rings the festive bell. I'm in. We'll take my car."

"Do you have something against riding vintage?" When I bought my house for the back taxes, it had come part and parcel with all the contents which included a seventies model Buick that I nicknamed Sally Forth.

"I like to drive. It's probably a control thing. Plus I have four-wheel drive and it's supposed to start snowing in the late afternoon. Just in case we're not back, I want to be in the car most likely to make the drive."

How could I argue with her logic?

At the town office, where Martha Tipton and her cronies had gathered to coordinate their efforts, we walked in on an argument.

"No, no, no. Honestly, Patricia, you just never listen. Sweet potatoes go in the turkey boxes, not the ones with ham. How hard is that to remember?"

"Go suck an egg, why don't you?" Deliberately, Patricia dropped two sweet potatoes in one of the boxes containing a ham. "I like sweet potatoes with ham, and there's enough to go around anyway. Who put you in charge of deciding what foods go with each other?"

I heard Patrea snort just before I waded in and diffused the situation like a pro. To be fair, it wasn't my first time with these two women, and since I'd been pitching in and using my contacts to help the town, Martha thought I walked on water. Which was why she took me aside.

"I was thinking," she said, "about that poor murdered girl. She has family in town, and I know her father's all alone up in Hackinaw, which doesn't fall strictly in with our efforts to help those in town who might need some extra this season. But I took the liberty of putting together a box for him anyway."

"That's so nice of her." Martha shivered when Amber popped in a bit too close.

"Do you think you could be the one to take it to him? I'd do it myself, but I'm worried about getting back ahead of the storm." As well she should be. On a sunny summer day, Martha might wind her car up to a solid thirty-five miles an hour in a fifty-five zone. In winter, she kept it under twenty. At that speed, she'd take half the day to drive to Hackinaw and back, and half the day was already gone.

I cast a glance at Patrea, who nodded. "Of course, we'd be happy to."

"Okay then, that's settled. You girls drive safe. You're a true treasure." Martha patted me on the arm. "Since you're going that way, could you also drop a box with Barbara

Dexter at the Bide-A-Way? She's still feeling poorly, so we put her on the list."

Without waiting for an answer, Martha pressed one of the ham boxes into Patrea's arms and, as a finishing touch, popped a Santa hat on each of our heads.

"That woman is a force of nature," Patrea said as she tossed her Santa hat on the back seat. "She's got you under her thumb."

I shrugged. "Maybe so, but it works in our favor this time, I suppose." But I dreaded an hour-long drive with Amber chattering away in the back seat. Too many chances to slip up and reveal her presence to Patrea. "We'll get a chance to talk to Amber's father. Plus the lake's pretty this time of year. Shouldn't take more than a couple of hours to drive up and back."

My prediction would have been true, except that when we got to the Bide-A-Way, we found Barbara attempting to clean room number four, and in far worse shape than she'd been before.

"Why didn't you call us for more help?" I probably should have thought to check on her.

"I'm fine. Just moving a little slow is all."

Patrea huffed out a breath. "You're not fine. You're shaking like a leaf, and I'd be willing to bet your head is pounding." She'd felt the same way during her bout of the flu. "You go back in the office and we'll finish up the cleaning."

Between us, we practically forced Barbara into compliance. "Have you been taking your elderberry syrup?"

"Ran out."

My eyebrows shot up. "I brought you enough to last two people a month. How much were you taking?"

"Oh, a slug here and there. Tastes good poured over ice cream."

Out of the corner of my eye, I noticed Patrea biting her lip.

"Worked pretty good on the flu, too. I thought I was over the worst of it, but I ran out and now I feel like hammered dirt again. Doctor said it's the flu. Drink plenty of fluids, take painkillers and cough syrup. Blah, blah, blah. Can only treat the symptoms."

Once we had her settled, I shot off a text to Jacy who answered right back. "Leandra will be over in an hour or so with tea and essential oils to go along with the elderberry. This time, take everything as directed, and you'll be feeling better in no time at all."

"Expect I will. Pretty near had it gone before. Else I drank enough not to care anymore. That stuff has a nice kick to it."

"That it does," Patrea said. "Was it just the one room to clean, or were there more?"

"Only the one. Miss princess from the news stayed a night in three, but all she done was complain about everything."

I didn't have to verify she meant Mia because, her voice hoarse from coughing, Barb still managed to do a pretty good impression of the reporter. "The decor is so outdated, and what's the thread-count on these sheets? Like fifty or something. Don't you have any hyper allergenic pillows?"

This time Patrea couldn't hold back the snort.

Barb shook her head. "Best way to deal with people like her is to play dumb. They either get to feelin' sorry for you, or they get pissed off and leave."

"And I bet I know which camp Mia landed in," I said.

"Well, she did leave, but I don't think my playing dumb was what pushed her over the edge. I think she got tired of chasing after the fellow in four, because he wasn't having any of it."

Finally, some good gossip.

"She's pretty cute," I said, "doesn't seem like the type a man would turn down."

145

"This one did, right enough. Anyway, thanks for the box. Told Martha we didn't need charity, but she said it wasn't charity to keep my sneezing butt away from the grocery store, just a general service to the entire community. Can't see how a body could argue with that."

Privately, I agreed with Martha, and I made a note to take a dose of preventive medicine when I got home. Possibly on ice cream.

"I see why you came back here," Patrea said when we went outside. "There's a real sense of family among the town community. It must be comforting to know there are people you can count on if something goes wrong, or even if you just need a helping hand."

"Sure there is," I agreed with her. "But the flip side is that you have an entire town full of people who think they're entitled to not only know your personal business, but talk about it."

Sadly, Lance Colby wasn't in his room when we knocked on the door. I'd have liked the chance to talk to him. As before, he'd tidied up before he left for wherever he spent his days—probably staking out my house—so there wasn't a lot to do. I carried clean towels into the bathroom and wiped everything down with disinfectant while Patrea stripped the bed.

On my way back out, I tripped over what proved to be Patrea's legs.

"What are you doing on the floor?" I couldn't see her past the armload of dirty towels. "Are you hurt?"

"I wasn't until you kicked me."

A fair point.

"It wasn't intentional." I dumped the towels on the cart outside, and when I came back, she was still on the floor. "What are you doing down there, anyway?" I hunkered down to peer under the bed, but all I saw was darkness.

"Most hotels go for platform beds these days. Keeps guests from losing stuff underneath and is easier to clean. This place hasn't been updated since the disco era."

"I can see that for myself, but it doesn't explain why you're on the floor."

Patrea shimmied and wiggled her way deeper until half her body was under the bed. "Okay, pull me out."

Sighing, I grabbed her by the ankles and gave a yank. When her face finally came into view again, she was smiling like it was half-off day at Prada. "Look what I found." She waved a shiny pink phone case in the air. "Battery's dead, but I'm betting when we charge it up, we'll find it belongs to Amber."

"We should turn that over to Ernie, but I vote we make sure it's Ambers before we do." If she'd ever show up when I needed her and not just when it wasn't convenient, I could save time and ask her. "Do you have a charger in your car?"

Patrea examined the phone's charge port. "Not for this type, but there must be a quick stop or something between here and Hackinaw. We'll pick one up."

"I know just the place, and while we're there, I'll buy you a slice. They get their pizza from Bertino's."

"With the special sauce?" Patrea spoke in the fervent tones of a true Bertino's addict.

"The regular, but it's almost as good."

We hurried to finish, but it was creeping up on two o'clock when we finally took the road north with the mystery phone charging and the car smelling of pepperoni and spices.

"If you hadn't hooked me on the fancy stuff, I'd have said this was one of the best slices I've ever eaten." Patrea polished off the last bite of crust while I keyed Amber's father's address into the GPS app on my phone.

"It doesn't suck," I agreed. "Looks like we don't have to drive all the way down to the lake. He lives up on the hill just before you pitch down into town."

Two hours before full dark with only a few small clouds scudded across the sky on a deepening breeze, I figured, left us plenty of time to get there and back ahead of any change in the weather. At least I was half right.

# CHAPTER 21

"Doesn't look like he's home," Patrea leaned close to the steering wheel to get a better look at the house and check for any signs of life. "What should we do? Leave the box on the doorstep?"

The temperature dropped a couple of degrees, so I knew Amber was there before she spoke in a grim tone. "He's home. The medical examiner released my body today, so he had to go in and make arrangements at the funeral home."

"His car's here." I said. "Why don't we knock on the door just in case he's inside." Without waiting for an argument, I got out and made my way up the front steps.

The revitalization plan for Hackinaw hadn't included provisions for homeowners, so the homes in the older sections of town all looked a bit dated. This one, with a little sag to the porch and peeling paint around the window frames, could have used a little work. Still, these turn of the century homes had been built to last through harsh winters and the strong winds blowing off the lake.

With Amber and Patrea bringing up the rear, I pulled open the storm door and peeked through the narrow window set in the center of the one behind it.

"There's a light on in the back." I applied my knuckles to the painted metal and waited. After a few moments passed with no movement inside, I knocked again.

"See, there's no one here."

"One more time." I rapped harder.

"Hold your horses," a man's voice called out, and after almost another full minute, Amber's father came into view. Somewhere in his mid-fifties, his shuffling gait made him seem older. "What do you want?" He approached, but didn't open the door.

"Mr. Hale, we've brought you a care package from the folks in Mooselick River, and we wanted to offer our condolences on the loss of your daughter. May we come in?"

"You knew my Amber?" The poor man looked at me through the glass.

"Hardly anyone has come here since I died." Amber popped her head through the door, her nose ending up a fraction of an inch from mine. The sudden chill almost made me sneeze.

"I think people aren't sure what to say," she said. "Or else it's like they're worried his bad luck will rub off on them, or something."

"He looks lonely," I whispered to Patrea, but she'd gone back for the box of goodies.

"Thanks for coming." He opened the door. "Tell me, how did you know my girl?"

*She hounded me for days and then my friend found her body*—while technically true seemed like a cruel answer. I took some pleasure in the fact that the always-right Patrea also hadn't realized coming here might open up a can of worms.

"Be careful what you say, he's fragile right now." All the cockiness gone, Amber sounded sad. "This is a good thing you're doing. He turned down my aunt's offer to spend Christmas with her family. I hate to think of him alone right now."

Fragile though he might be, Mr. Hale seemed pleased to have company. I'd wanted him to invite us in, but now that he had, I didn't have the heart to ask the hard questions.

Patrea come through the door and saved me from having to tell him who I was.

Tipping the box down to show him the contents, she said, "I hope you like turkey instead of ham. Can we help you put these things away?"

He waved his hand toward the doorway behind and toward his left.

"Thank you, but you can just put the box on the table. I'll take care of it later. Will you be coming to Amber's service? It's the day after Christmas." Mr. Hale's voice went hoarse with the effort to hold back tears. "I can't believe she's gone. My poor girl. How did you know her again? Did you work with her at the station?"

I hoped my winter hat covered enough of my face he wouldn't recognize me from the news reports. "No, I'm sorry, I didn't. I only met Amber a few days before she died."

"Oh." His shoulders sagged.

"It's okay, Daddy. I'm still here." Amber moved close, whispered in his ear.

I watched for him to shiver in the chill of her nearness; he leaned closer to her, a hint of a smile teasing his mouth. Mr. Hale hadn't shaved in a day or two and he'd buttoned his cardigan wrong, but that smile left me no doubt he felt her presence.

"Then you must come in and let me tell you all about her."

I exchanged a glance with Patrea, and followed him into the living room. Framed photos took up an entire wall. Many featured Amber at various ages, the rest professional quality outdoor shots of the lake and surroundings.

Drawn to take a closer look at the scenics, Patrea said, "These are lovely."

"Tell him he should have them made into prints and sell them in one of the local shops." Amber's order bordered on breaking the messages to family rule, but she was right.

"Are these your work, Mr. Hale?"

"Call me Ned. Yes, everyone needs a hobby."

151

"If you ever decide have some prints made from them, I know a gallery owner who would be happy to sell them for you."

Ned waved the idea away. "You sound like my daughter."

I wonder why.

"Mr. Hale," I began, and when he gave me a look, amended, "Ned, do you know if Amber was seeing anyone? Or if maybe she'd met someone recently? Did she mention a man named Chris?"

"No, there was no one serious. Not on her end anyway. I think young Lance might have wanted more, but Amber's mother and me," Ned shook his head sadly. "Things didn't turn out so well with us, and my baby suffered for it. She never could settle down with anyone. Couldn't let herself trust enough, and I blame myself for failing to show her any different."

"It wasn't his fault." I don't know if ghosts cry exactly, but Amber sniffled. "He lived for me and I don't think he even realizes he let that stand in the way of finding someone. Now he'll be alone for the rest of his life, and I'll never be able to tell him he was the best father in the world."

I sighed, and knowing I'd have to explain myself to Patrea later, went ahead and smashed my rule about messages to bits...or at least I knocked the edges off.

"Like I said, I didn't know Amber well, but she attributed her success to having a supportive father. She loved you, and if she could be here right now, I'm sure that's what she'd tell you."

"Close enough." Amber faded away.

Something he'd said popped back into my head. "You knew Lance?" Finally, some information that might help.

"Nice kid. Showed up here the day after it happened. Been coming around every day to see if I need anything. Sits with me awhile. Doesn't talk much, though."

"That's good of him." Patrea caught my eye and nodded toward the door. "Now, if you'll excuse us, we need to head back." I hated to leave him there alone again, but I didn't see another option. On the way out, I stopped for a closer look at one of the photos. "Your wife?"

A woman who looked a lot like Amber held a tow-headed toddler on her lap. Ned had captured the curve of the child's cheek, and every wrinkle in the pudgy hand that reached toward the locket dangling on a chain from the woman's neck. Both were smiling.

Ned nodded. "Amber hated that she took after her mom."

Patrea went on ahead while I fished a Curated Collections card from my purse. "Call my friend. Amber was right, people deserve to see your work."

He took the card, but I doubted he'd ever use it.

"She comes to see me, you know." He all but whispered it. "My Amber."

"Yes, I know."

# CHAPTER 22

Patrea started the car, and while we waited for it to warm up a little, turned in her seat to look at me.

"That was a nice thing you did in there."

I blinked at her. "You think so?" I hadn't actually lied, but Patrea couldn't know that.

"I do," she said.

"It was." Amber chimed in from the back seat. "Thank you."

All I could do was nod my head as Patrea reversed onto the street and drove into the rapidly deepening twilight. A mile out of town, I reached for the cell phone that had been charging for almost two hours by then, and thumbed the on button. Bothered by the sudden light of the display, Patrea held up a shielding hand.

"Turn that the other way, or reduce the brightness."

"Oh, sorry, I can turn it off until we get home." I reached to do just that.

"No, just don't aim it at me. I'm dying to know if it's Amber's phone."

I couldn't tell by the lock screen which only showed the time and date. Swiping my finger to unlock brought up a box demanding a pass code.

"Well, I guess that's a bust. We need a three-digit code for it to unlock."

Amber's breath...or whatever it is a ghost exudes...felt icy cold on the back of my neck. "It's mine. The code is—" she trailed off.

There are rules, apparently, that ghosts must follow. The worst of them is not being able to speak the name of their killer. Amber hadn't seen hers, so that was a moot point in this case, but I kept waiting to hit on something that violated the scope of the no-talky rule. Maybe her phone password had fallen into the dead zone.

When I glanced into the back seat, Amber was gone. Just great.

"Well, that's what...720 possible number combinations." Patrea did the math in her head. "Shouldn't take more than a week to figure it out."

"I'm impressed you came up with that number so quickly."

Leaning forward to check before she pulled out onto the main road, Patrea shrugged. "I'm good with numbers, but it's not a skill I wanted to make a living with."

"Five, two, and eight." Amber was back.

"Okay, then," I pretended to study the phone, "Assuming she chose the code instead of just using random numbers, I'm thinking she'd use the number five since it's her station's call number."

Patrea tapped her fingers on the steering wheel while she recalculated. "That drops it down to 150. More manageable, but it will still take some time to try them all."

Since the numbers were five, two, and eight, it wouldn't take as long as Patrea thought. "I'll start with the five since it makes sense she'd use that one, and work my way through. Maybe we'll get lucky."

Though my fingers itched to just type in the code, I started with five, zero, zero.

Looking down, I wasn't paying attention to the road until I heard the wipers come on. We'd run into the storm, and it was a dilly. Thick ice coated the wipers as they worked to clear the layer of wet, sloppy snow that fell like a blanket.

"Whoa. That came on quick."

155

"Like running into a wall." Patrea hit the button on the rear defrost. "One minute it was clear, the next...this mess. Bless the person who invented all-wheel drive."

Squinting out the window, I tried to figure out where we were. "I can't even see beyond the snowbanks. A night like this, you could go right past the turnoff to town. Any idea where we are now?" I put Amber's phone down and pulled out my own, unlocked the screen, and tapped on the navigation app.

"GPS can't get a signal."

"The last sign I saw said Harris Road. If that helps."

It did. "How long ago?"

"About a mile before we hit the storm, so three or four minutes." The sound of the wipers seemed loud as I tried to calculate distances.

"Okay, then. We have a left turn coming up soon, but before that is a sharp bend to the right, so you'd better slow down."

Patrea huffed. "We're doing under twenty now, because I can't see much past the end of the hood and the defroster is barely keeping the windows clear. If I go any slower, we're going to freeze in place."

She rotated shoulders tense from the strain even though we'd only been in the storm for a few minutes. By the time another five inched past, mine were feeling the strain as well.

"Okay. Road's bending hard to the right. How much farther?"

"Half a mile," I said. "Give or take. I'm not good with distances."

After another minute, Patrea eased toward the left, hugged the bank on that side. "You watch ahead for oncoming lights while I look for the turnoff."

Because, you know, driving down the wrong side of the road during a blinding snowstorm is my idea of a good time. Lady luck was on our side, or maybe she drove on the right, I have no idea, but either way, we made the turn without incident.

"It's a straight shot from here."

I no sooner got the words out of my mouth than Patrea spun the wheel hard, sending us into a skid. I caught a flash of someone standing in the road as we spun past, and heard Patrea's vicious curse over the shushing sound of snow under our tires. While my stomach lurched, she wrestled the car under control, and we came to a stop with the hood pointed back the way we had come.

"Freaking moron. She could have been killed."

"Who was that? I only caught a glimpse of someone when we went by." Maybe in an hour or two, my heart rate would return to normal.

Patrea began to drive slowly forward. "Mia James."

"You didn't hit her, did you?"

The wipers had too much ice on them to be effective, so Patrea opened her window, caught hers on the upswing, and banged it on the windshield to clear it. "No, I didn't hit her, but she's damn lucky."

Visibility was so bad we were almost upon her again before we saw Mia standing next to where she'd buried her car in the snowbank. Her tracks were filling up fast, but it looked like she'd been on her way out of town.

Pulling up alongside her, Patrea powered down both our windows, waved impatiently toward the wipers on my side. I took the hint and banged mine clean to match hers while she talked to Mia.

"Are you hurt?"

Mia looked stunned, but I couldn't see any signs of physical trauma from where I sat. "Bumped my head against the side window when I hit the bank, but otherwise, I think I'm okay. I thought you were going to kill me, though."

"I'm still tempted to, but you'd better lock up your car and let us give you a ride back to town."

157

"You're a big girl, don't you think between the two of you, you could push me out?" Mia proved her utter lack of people skills.

"Get in or don't." Patrea gritted out from between clenched teeth. "Up to you, but decide now."

"I'll call Bennie over at Pine Tree Auto and if he's not already out on a tow call, we can drop her off at his place on our way into town." I refused to speak to Mia and thought it might be best to limit the time she and Patrea spent together. "We're going right by there anyhow and it's close."

A root canal would be more fun than five minutes in an enclosed space with Mia.

"Fine," she rolled her eyes, and I saw Patrea's foot move off the brake. Honestly, I couldn't blame her for the urge to leave Mia standing in the snow, but I didn't think either of us wanted her on our conscience.

Sighing, Mia settled into the back seat, pulled off her hat, then flapped her wrist at Patrea. "Let's go, then."

Jaw clenched, eyes facing forward, Patrea drove as fast as the weather allowed while I made the call.

"He's a half hour out, but his wife says you can stay there until he shows up."

Mia sniffed and made a nasty comment about Mooselick River being a backwater town under her breath. Patrea sucked in air to come back with a hot retort.

"She's not worth it," I muttered.

Leaning forward in the seat, Mia spoke loudly in my ear. "Off the record, you knew about the other woman, right? I mean, your husband does your friend like that, you have to have some idea what's going on."

"No comment."

"I said off the record. Jeez."

Mia sat back and, counting the minutes until we could be rid of her, I stared out the window trying to get my bearings. The dropping temperature had begun to turn the sloppy wet clumps into smaller, harder flakes that ticked against the windshield.

Between gusts, I thought I caught sight of the sign announcing we'd crossed the town line, but it was difficult to be certain. "If we're where I think we are, you should see a driveway just ahead, on your side."

She did, and we turned in, passed the snowed-over hulks of a couple of old wreckers, and dropped Mia off at Bennie's doorstep.

"She didn't even say thank you," Patrea steamed. "I could totally understand the motive if someone had murdered her instead of Amber."

"I'll be glad when all of this mess with Paul blows over and I can go back to my boring, backwater life."

Ghosts flitting in and out of the house might not qualify as boring, but other parts of my life did. I liked my job well enough, but the biggest excitement in a month had been when the furnace at one of the units went out. I'd had to roust Tony in the middle of the night to check on it, and drop off a couple of electric heaters to keep the kiddies warm while he waited for parts. I managed rental properties for the most conscientious landlord on the planet. Leo Hanson paid me well, but mine was a fairly drama-free job.

"You really don't miss the designer clothes and gala events?"

Somehow, I didn't think any of those were high on Patrea's list of fun activities, either, but I gave the question due thought before answering.

"I guess I don't. All the glitz and glamor are fine once in a while, but I grew up in a different world, and Paul's lifestyle never felt entirely real to me." I hadn't told anyone that before.

Apparently, my confession touched a nerve.

"Growing up with money," a chill threaded through Patrea's tone, "didn't make me less real than you. That's a lousy stereotype."

159

"I didn't mean it that way. I wasn't generalizing, I meant Paul specifically. Our house was nice, but not too nice because he was careful about appearances. He played it off as though he had simpler tastes and didn't care about all the trappings. Looking back, I can see the lie."

Appeased, Patrea wanted to know more. Surprisingly, there was more of that *more* than I'd realized.

"His tastes ran toward expensive cars, but when it came time to buy, he always chose something that fit in with what the neighbors owned. There was the decorator who came in with a storyboard for what she wanted to do with the rooms. Lush fabrics, custom furniture—the kinds of rooms that end up in magazine spreads. She was not too happy with him when he sent her back to redo all the rooms people might see and make them look less expensive.

"Patrea frowned. "Keeping down with the Joneses."

"Exactly. That's what I meant about his lifestyle not feeling real. Especially when, on the flip side, he spent lavishly on things no one would normally see, and also on clothes. Now, I'm wondering if those habits were more than eccentricities."

Snow still fell in gusts and sheets when we passed the dim glow of the first streetlight on the edge of town. Staring into the dark and driving snow has a mesmerizing effect and I wouldn't have been one bit surprised to look in the mirror and see my eyes with those spinning cartoon swirls in them.

Two seconds later, Patrea wondered, "You think Mrs. Petrakis has anyone on for delivery?"

"I don't do—" I started to say delivery, then thought the better of it. I didn't want to cook, and I didn't want to stop, either. "Probably. But can we have something besides pizza?"

"Order anything you want, as long as it comes with breadsticks and the special sauce."

Once we got back to my house Patrea shrugged off her coat, then headed upstairs to change into jammie pants and a loose sweater while I took Molly out for a game of bite the

160

snow. One of her favorites, the game was simple. I shoveled off the steps and walkway while Molly leaped and snapped at the snow flying off the end of the shovel. She doubled my workload with her antics and ended up with tiny snowballs clinging to the few bits of her fur long enough for the snow to find purchase. Mostly along the underside of her tail.

I'd worked off most of the shoulder strain, and she was panting by the time I cleared the path. "You look ridiculous, you silly dog, but who could resist that face?"

Getting both of us dried and Molly fed took up the rest of the time until the delivery driver rang the doorbell with our food. I'd hated to call anyone out in that weather, but it was only a short distance and Patrea gave the guy an outrageous tip for his efforts.

Sticking out her tongue, Patrea licked an errant drop of sauce from the corner of her mouth. "I'm going to miss this when I go home. I wonder if they sell it by the gallon so I can stock up."

"Not that I'm aware," I grinned. "You'll just have to buy twenty or thirty orders of breadsticks and freeze the containers of sauce."

"Don't think I'm not tempted."

We ended the night with another Christmas movie. A madcap comedy without romantic overtones to keep Patrea from brooding over Chris.

# CHAPTER 23

Over coffee the next morning, my phone buzzed to signal an incoming text.

*OMG*

Jacy followed that up with a whole line of emojis—hearts, stars, a house, a couple dancing.

"I think Jacy's closing on her house today." I flashed the screen at Patrea. "Nothing like leaving it until the last minute before Christmas."

"Happy Christmas Eve Eve to her." With her mug, Patrea toasted the good news.

"You know what this means, don't you?"

She quirked an eyebrow.

"In a minute, I'm going to get a text saying Jacy wants to move a couple of boxes over, and do I want to come see the new house. I've seen it. I went with her to look at it several times before they decided, but that's code."

"Code for—?"

"Code for she's going to rent a truck from the hardware store and move everything in today." My phone buzzed again. "Right on schedule. You don't have to help, but I do. Jacy's family, so I'll go play pack mule for a couple of hours."

"I'll go. I want to see, too." I should have known she would. The minute I mentioned a new house, her eyes lit up and I remembered who I was talking to. "She's moving into a real house, right? Something with a little age to it, and some character."

I nodded.

"Wait, how much stuff does she have, and how did she manage to get a closing this close to the holiday?"

"Oh, I'm pretty sure Jacy threatened to have her mother curse someone if they didn't close before Christmas."

"If her curses are as good as her flu remedies, I'd rather not be on the receiving end of one."

Leandra was a healer, so to anyone who knew her well, the threat was an empty one.

"They're in a small, one-bedroom apartment, so they don't have much, but it's a walk-up. Still, Brian has four brothers to do the heavy lifting and Jacy started packing the first time they were supposed to close, so they've been living with just the bare essentials since the first of the month. Shouldn't take long."

Another text hit my phone.

*Signing papers now. See you in an hour.*

An hour gave us time to eat and get Molly settled.

"What does she need? I want to stop on the way and get her a housewarming gift."

"Today?"

"Well, yeah. Why not?"

I hated to remind Patrea where she was. "It's Sunday in Mooselick River. Your options are the hardware store, the bait shop, and the grocery store. It's not like she's registered."

She waved her hand impatiently. "The hardware store carries stuff, right? Like small appliances, and whatever."

"More whatever than stuff, but sure, I guess we could find something there."

"Good. Then shake a leg. We'll leave a little early."

Not early enough, it seemed, because by the time Patrea had burned her way through the kitchenware section of the hardware store, we pulled up behind a halfway-unloaded moving truck.

The Cape Cod style house, painted a cheerful, dark blue with white trim, looked as cozy on the outside as it did on the inside. If I closed my eyes, I could picture Jacy's future here, with a swing set behind the picket fence and a grill going in the backyard.

Even from the outside, the house felt happy.

"Hey, Brian." I managed to snag the new homeowner for a hug as I passed him headed back for more boxes and teased, "Didn't your mother tell you to be careful about making faces like that? It might stick."

The smile on his face couldn't get wider, and I had to look down to make sure his feet were still touching the ground. The last time I'd seen Brian this happy was when Jacy came through the doors at the back of the church in all her wedding finery.

"Jacy's inside. Make her sit down for ten minutes if you can."

"I'll give it a shot."

I had to drag Patrea away from examining the pattern in the cedar shake siding on the porch. "That's a sawtooth pattern over rounded tab shingles. Very creative even if this porch is a later addition." She could talk house styles all day long and half the time it sounded like she spoke a different language.

Inside, I followed the sound of Jacy's lilting voice to the kitchen where she was stacking plates in a cabinet. When she laid eyes on me, she squealed and did a somewhat ungainly happy dance.

"Guess what! The real estate broker felt so bad about it taking so long, he paid for a professional cleaning service to come in. They swept, mopped, and wiped everything down so all we have to do is unpack."

Gently, I nudged Jacy toward the closest seat. "Here, I'll do that. Patrea's got something for you."

"Sorry it's not wrapped. The hardware store didn't have anything except for something more suitable for a five-year-old boy, and Christmas paper."

My ploy to get Jacy into a chair lasted two seconds because she jumped back up to give Patrea a hug. "You didn't have to get us anything," she grinned, "but I'm glad you did. I just love presents."

"Then, sit down and open it."

"Brian told you to make me sit. He's been doing that with everyone, but since my ankles are beginning to look like tree trunks, I'll oblige." Jacy sat and accepted what looked like a balled-up plastic bag. "My goodness, this is heavy." She unwrapped the plastic.

"It's a cast-iron garlic roaster." Face reddening, Patrea jumped in before Jacy could say thank you.

"Of course, it is. I knew that." Tears ran down Jacy's face, and when she sniffled, Patrea looked at me with panic written all over her face.

"Jacy." I leaned down to make eye contact. "Honey, what's the matter?"

"I can take it back."

I wasn't sure which woman looked more miserable.

"Don't you dare," Jacy wailed. "I love it."

"Then why are you crying?" Patrea beat me to the question.

"Because it's so nice, and it's the first gift for my new house." Neither of those seemed worth a bout of tears. "And I've got pregnancy hormones."

Well, that explained things.

After the tears dried up, with Jacy directing, Patrea and I made short work of unpacking the boxes labeled: Kitchen. We'd moved on to the bedroom when Neena showed up.

"Be careful what you say. She cries at the drop of a hat," Patrea warned.

"What else is new?" Neena pitched right in by hanging clothes in the closet. "Yesterday, she cried because we had extra toilet paper at the shop."

"Don't." Jacy held up a hand. "You'll get me started again."

Neena held up both hands in surrender. "Consider the topic dead."

"Speaking of the dead," Jacy picked up the segue and ran with it. "Did you hear Mia James is missing?"

"How is that speaking of the dead?"

"Well, she worked with Amber Hale, didn't she? So that's one person dead, and people are saying Mia's probably dead, too."

This was news to me, and judging by the nonplussed look on Patrea's face, she was thinking the same thing I was. "When did all this happen? We saw her last night."

"Really?" Jacy said. "You might have been the last people to see her alive."

Great. Just what I needed. More scandal.

"I don't think so. We dropped her off at Pine Tree Auto with Bennie's wife to wait for him to come back so he could pull her car out of a snowbank." Which reminded me, I still had Amber's phone in my purse. In all the excitement and fatigue, we'd forgotten all about it. But now wasn't the time to pull it out, so it would have to wait until we had Jacy settled. "Besides, how can she be considered missing? It's been less than twenty-four hours. Isn't there a mandatory forty-eight before the police will let family file a missing persons report?"

"That's a myth," Patrea said. "Mostly perpetuated by television. Police will look at a person's daily patterns and often will put out a BOLO or even file a missing persons within hours. How did they figure out she was missing?"

"Oh, easy." Jacy applied a steak knife to the tape on a box of blankets. "She didn't show up for work this morning."

"Hey, maybe she got lucky with the hot dancer guy." Neena didn't realize she'd stuck her foot in it until I caught her attention and nodded toward Patrea. "Oh, sorry! But I saw her talking to him at the grocery store yesterday afternoon. Did you know there wasn't a loaf of bread left in the place at least an hour before the snow started? And the milk cooler was almost empty, too."

While Patrea went completely still, Jacy filled the awkward silence. "I know. What do people do with all that bread and milk? I could see it if there was a run on peanut butter and jelly, but milk goes bad if the power is out, so it makes no sense."

"How did they look?"

Neena mistook Patrea's question. "Like empty shelves."

"No, Chris and Mia. Was he flirting? Or touching her?"

"I—"

"Never mind, I don't want to know."

When Neena started to explain, Patrea held up a hand. "Really, I don't want to know." She didn't say much after that, but her speed at unpacking went up a notch—landing at a level just below violence.

The truck emptied, Brian and one of his brothers were putting the crib together while the other two hooked up the entertainment system. From the nursery came mild cursing, and a discussion revolving around whether there were six bolts in the bag marked A or only five.

With so many willing hands, another hour saw the boxes flattened and carried to the garage.

"It looks empty, doesn't it? All this extra space. It's bigger than I thought. Or maybe I didn't think too much about it, but we don't have nearly enough stuff." Settling on a soft chair in the living room, Jacy plopped her feet on the matching foot stool.

Since I'd planned to take her on a free shopping trip through the furniture laden addition on my house, we'd remedy some of that problem with her Christmas gift.

"Won't take long." Neena grinned at her business partner. "She has a pile of things in the storeroom already earmarked for personal purchase."

"One of the perks of owning your own business." Jacy wasn't repentant in the least. "Cherry picking the things I want for myself makes the whole thing more fun."

167

Since Patrea had gone largely silent, and worse, looked to be fuming, I figured it was time to get her out of there so she could explode in private.

"Congratulations on the new place. We'll do game night here as soon as you're settled in." I'd have liked to stay a little longer in case Jacy needed more help, but she'd seen Patrea's face. The one thing you can count on with Jacy is her empathy. It runs deep and wide and you don't have to be a lifelong friend to trigger it because Patrea already had. Jacy wouldn't begrudge me not being there for the rest of her special moving day.

"I'm feeling pretty settled now. Or maybe I'm just too pregnant to move," she waved us out the door.

# CHAPTER 24

At the end of Jacy's street, Patrea turned right instead of left, and even though I know where we were going, I had to ask. "You know my house is the other way, right?"

"Yep."

I didn't have Chris's phone number and I probably wouldn't have warned him if I did, because you know, solidarity sister and all that, but I did feel a little sorry for him. Patrea in a full-blown fury was one thing, but this was cold rage, and I figured that had to be worse.

Maybe she wouldn't kill him. Maybe she'd only maim him a little. One could only hope, but I didn't like his chances.

"You're sure you don't want to—"

Eyes straight ahead, Patrea said, "Nope."

At least I tried.

The rest of the trip to Evergreen Farm passed in brooding silence on her side of the car, worried silence on mine, and ended when we spun through a small drift of loose snow in front of the house. Patrea knew where she was going, and left me to either sit and wait or follow in her wake.

Decisions, decisions.

She'd taken the keys and it was too cold to sit in the car, so I followed her. Old farmhouses in Maine often grew along with the families that lived in them, so they tend to be a hodgepodge of sections, and this one was no different. To feed livestock more easily during brutal winters, farmers built their barns close to the houses and connected them with shed-like areas to use as convenient walkways.

Patrea disappeared through the door to one of these sections, and I hurried after to keep from getting lost. Not that there was any chance of that with her shouting at the top of her lungs.

"Chris Evergreen, you haul your sorry ass out from whatever corner you're hiding in. I've got something to say to you." The door she banged open led into the kitchen, and I heard a faint exclamation from somewhere deeper in the house.

A few seconds later, Chris walked into the room carrying a flannel shirt and wearing nothing but a pair of jeans. Fully-clothed, the man was a treat for the eyes; half-naked, he was Christmas and Halloween all rolled into one. No wonder Patrea jumped on him when she had the chance.

"Put on a shirt," she said while I looked for a place to stand that wasn't in the line of fire. "I can't have this conversation with you like that."

I ducked around the corner and sat down at the kitchen table where I could hear, but not see the conversation play out.

"That's what I was doing when you started yelling at the top of your lungs." Chris didn't raise his voice, and his tone was as neutral as Switzerland. I heard the rustle of cloth and excuse me if I pictured him shrugging on the flannel with a ripple of muscles. Some things, once seen, cannot be unseen. This time, I was okay with that.

"What happened," Patrea slammed hands on her hips, "to Mia James?"

Chris blinked in confusion.

"Who?"

"Mia James. You were seen talking to her outside the grocery store just before the storm hit yesterday." Patrea described Mia.

Shaking his head, Chris stared at her. "You mean the woman who asked me where the closest hotel that wasn't, and I quote, 'decorated by some delusional housewife from the stone age'. I pointed her toward Hackinaw and warned her about the storm."

Well, that cleared up a few questions.

Then Patrea took the conversation into the personal zone.

"Did you mean any of the things you said to me? Or was all that business about there not being anyone for years just a line to get me into bed?"

If it was, it was the cheesiest line in the history of lines.

"Believe what you want to believe, Patrea. I didn't see you rushing to defend me when Everly practically accused me of murder."

That got me on my feet, and I poked my head around the corner.

"I did not." Except I sort of had, in my head, anyway. "Or not seriously."

"Shut up, Everly." On that point, at least, they agreed. I shut up and went back to my seat in the kitchen while the battle raged on.

From my partially objective point of view, these were two people with very similar insecurities. People who had both been burned, and were understandably gun-shy about committing to a relationship. Two people trying to come together despite all of those insecurities.

Paul hadn't cared enough to fight with me like this. There hadn't been enough heat or passion in him for more than a snide comment or a withering stare. Funny how remembering that about him didn't really hurt anymore.

"I danced with Amber, nothing more."

"He's not lying." Amber popped in across from me. "And he was really nice when he turned me down. That doesn't happen very often, and it made me think about some of my choices. I might have made some changes if all of this," she gestured to her ghostly body, "hadn't happened."

Chris continued, "A woman like that gives off signals to every man she sees because to her, love and lust mean the same. She offered me her body to use in any way I chose. I wanted more."

Even from the kitchen I heard the whoosh of Patrea taking in a breath. "So did I, but I guess we're both doomed to disappointment."

Chris realized his mistake. "I didn't mean from Amber. I danced with her. I dance with a lot of women. I never take them home with me."

"I guess we both know better."

"One of us does. The other has trouble grasping nuances."

"You walked away without looking back. I think I'll do the same."

If I hadn't hurried to follow Patrea out, I think she might have left me there. I managed one backward look at Chris, but couldn't read anything from his expression.

I spent half the ride back to my house with Patrea glowering and Amber making inappropriate comments comparing the way Chris danced to the way he might do other things. Desperate to diffuse the tension, I fished through my purse and came up with Amber's phone.

"Do you remember where I left off with this?"

Not ready to be pulled out of the doldrums, Patrea shrugged. "No idea."

Good enough, I thought. "Somewhere around five, two, zero, maybe." I punched the numbers in.

My acting skills aren't even close to Oscar-worthy, but I think I did okay when, just as we passed the grocery store, I let out a whoop, and said, "We're in."

"Don't give up your day job for the bright lights of Hollywood." Amber poofed.

"Open it." Patrea perked up. "No, don't. Not while I'm driving. Just wait."

Since I'd been gone longer than planned, Molly needed to bleed off some energy with a romp in the snow while Patrea chomped at the bit. I will neither confirm nor deny that making her wait satisfied a minor need for payback. Making her wait while I heated water for tea, well, that one was just plain spite.

"Open up her messages first." Impatient, she reached over to brush my hand away and tap the icon herself. Smiling inwardly, I handed over the phone. At least she didn't look like she'd dropped her lollipop in the toilet anymore. "Looks like a lot of work stuff."

Patrea scrolled while I sipped my tea.

"Nope. More work stuff...now that's interesting." I set my cup on the table and nudged closer so I could see the screen. One look and I wished I hadn't. Patrea had found the icon for a popular dating app hidden in a nested folder. Though dating app probably wasn't the correct term. Hook-up hotline might be more appropriate.

"Is this a thing now?" I hadn't been married all that long, but it seemed as if dating had not only gone digital, but had taken a cruise into waters I wasn't prepared to wade in. "Sending a photo of your, um...stuff to someone before you've even met? People really do this?"

I held the proof in my hand, but still asked the dumb question.

"Well, they send pictures of someone's stuff, not necessarily their own. You know, hook 'em with a bratwurst, then when the time comes reveal the weenie and hope for the best."

I snorted and handed back the phone. "What happened to romance? If this is how it works now, I'm glad I decided to stay single."

It looked like Patrea had something to say on the subject, but she held back and returned scrolling through Amber's phone.

"Do you think one of her dates thought she'd promised...and I don't want to know if there's a female version of the bratwurst/weenie comparison...but maybe someone thought Amber promised something she didn't deliver."

"Doubtful, but if nothing else pops, we can revisit her matches."

Patrea went back to scrolling while online dating rocketed right to the top of my To Don't list. Contemplating that list, I'd fallen into a stupor when I felt the sofa bounce under me, and looked up to see Amber's phone on the coffee table and Patrea headed for the kitchen.

"Sorry, I glazed over for a minute there, I take it you didn't find anything."

"We already knew Lance had a bit of a thing for Amber, but he must have sent her a hundred photos he took of her. Candids mostly. Artsy stuff. Videos, too."

Right at home in my kitchen, Patrea put on a pot of water to boil, and then hunted through the fridge for the small blocks of Parmesan and Romano cheese I kept wrapped in plastic and stored in the back. Eggs and bacon joined the cheese on the counter.

Assuming she'd ask for my help if she wanted it, I went back to grab the phone and settled in at the table to swipe my way through far too many shots of Amber. Close-ups of her face from every angle, all taken, it seemed to me, without her knowledge.

"You're right. Lance might have missed his calling. He should be doing portraits for a living."

"I know, right?" Patrea transferred the pasta from the pot to the skillet she'd used to cook the bacon, added the cheese and eggs, then ladled in pasta water to make a creamy carbonara.

While we ate, I set the phone in the middle of the table and kept scrolling through the seemingly endless folder of images. "This bunch must have been taken at the station, there's Mia."

"Looking pissed off as usual," Patrea pointed out.

174

There were at least a dozen long shots of Amber speaking to co-workers, several with Mia glaring in the background. I scrolled past those and the first image in the next series made Patrea nearly choke on her pasta.

Eyes closed, head thrown back, hair flying, her body a study of sensuous curves, his arm flung around her waist, Amber danced with Chris.

It was already too late, but I swiped backwards so Patrea didn't have to look.

"It's okay," reaching over, she swiped through the entire series, studying Chris's face. "It's really okay."

She sounded cheerful.

"I'm sorry. This has to hurt."

The crazy woman grinned at me. "No, it's fine. Look at his face." She scrolled and pointed. "He's not even looking at her. Do you see it? A man gets a woman like that in his arms, dancing the sexy dance of hotness, and if he's interested, he's gonna at least check out her assets. I mean come on, there's an acre of cleavage right there, and he's not even looking."

"You're right. He's not."

"He wasn't lying to me. It was only dancing."

"Did I not say that already? I told you we only danced. Why is this a revelation?" Amber leaned in close enough to send a shiver over Patrea's skin.

I couldn't answer, but I did have questions, and I couldn't ask those at the moment, but maybe Amber wasn't the right person to ask.

"We know Lance had a thing for Amber, how do you think he felt seeing her like that?" Meanwhile, Patrea had scrolled through the series to get to the last image Lance had sent. Amber took one look and faded away. "She's wearing the same clothes she had on when we found her. Maybe he figured if he couldn't have her, no one could."

Nodding, I left the last few bites on my plate and went to find my phone. Keeping my eyes on Patrea, I dialed.

175

"Hey Barbara, it's Everly Dupree. You sound better today…can you tell me if the guy in four happens to be around?" The motel owner confirmed her renewed health and told me to hang on while she checked.

"Car's there, which is weird. He said he was planning to check out at one, but he's still here."

"Can you do me a favor? Don't go talk to him, but if he comes into the office, or if he leaves, can you call me? I need to talk to him, but it will take me fifteen minutes or so to get there."

"Sure." Barb agreed. "You'll explain later, though." It wasn't a question.

"I will. Just stall him if he tries to leave."

I jammed my feet into my boots, grabbed my coat, and followed Patrea to the car. "Roads aren't bad, we'll shave a minute or two off that fifteen." As soon as she hit the edge of town, she jammed on the gas while I kicked off my boots.

"What are you doing?"

"Was in a rush, put them on the wrong feet."

We made it in twelve, and pulled in next to the car parked in front of four. "Looks like he's still here."

"Let's do this, then." She reached the door first, banging on it and calling for Lance. We waited.

"Maybe that's not his car. Shouldn't it have the station logo on the side?"

"Probably his personal," Patrea banged again.

This time I heard a muffled sound from inside. "Something's wrong." I tried the knob, but it was locked. "Do you think we should break it down?" I wasn't sure we could, but people do remarkable things when the adrenaline gets pumping.

"I'd rather you didn't." I hadn't heard Barbara come out, but was grateful when she produced her keys and unlocked the door which swung wide to reveal Lance Colby, naked and shivering, both hands cuffed to the headboard, and silver tape

176

over his mouth. Above the tape, his eyes fluttered, but didn't fully open. He moaned again.

"Call Ernie." I tossed out the order and swiveled my head, searching for the bedspread to cover the poor man with. In his attempts to get free, it looked like he'd kicked it on the floor. Quickly, but without looking too closely to preserve whatever modesty he might possess, I tucked the bedspread around him while Patrea kicked the temp up on the room heater.

I could hear Barb talking to Ernie.

"No, he's not dead.... because he's breathing and his eyelids are fluttering. Just get over here, and call an ambulance while you're at it...damn fool." I hoped she made that last comment after Ernie hung up, but I wouldn't bet on it.

As gently as we could, with Patrea working from one side and me from the other, we tried to get the tape off Lance's mouth. He moaned a couple more times, and opened his eyes all the way once, but they were glassy.

"Drugged. I'd lay money on it," was Patrea's opinion, which was borne out by the med tech when the ambulance arrived just ahead of Ernie, who took a quick look at the scene, then unlocked the cuffs. While the medics worked on Lance, Ernie grilled the three of us for details on how and why we'd found Lance the way we did.

The set of Ernie's mouth told me plain enough that he wasn't too happy to find me there, but he kept his comments about it to himself for once and stuck to the facts.

"Can't say for sure without running bloodwork, but it looks like GHB, or maybe rohypnol. He's responsive to stimuli, but it'll be a few hours before he's coherent enough to talk. Even then, it's unlikely he'll remember much." The EMT gave Ernie a brief update.

Once the ambulance had gone, Ernie ran us through the details twice more, only this time, from the warmth of Barbara's office because, in her words, she wasn't in the mood for another bout of the plague. It took more than an hour before he was satisfied, we'd given him every detail, and almost another to assuage Barbara's curiosity.

# CHAPTER 25

"I could go for a beer," Patrea paused at the stop sign where turning left would take us to Cappy's and right would take us back home.

"And wings. I'm starving." On the way, I texted Neena who said she'd be happy to see to Molly, and even offered her services as driver should we overindulge.

"As long as they come with fries."

Our regular table occupied, we had to take one on the opposite end of the bar, near the restrooms.

Lance, of course, and the possible ways he might have ended up in his predicament, was the main topic of discussion over drinks. I nearly spit mine when Patrea offered the suggestion that Barb had decided to keep him as her love slave.

"That's a mental image that requires brain bleach to remove." But it was an amusing one that sent us into a fit of the giggles.

Patrea's laughter stopped abruptly, and when I turned to see why, locked eyes with Chris Evergreen.

"I'm sorry. We can leave. I'll tell Miranda to put the food in a to-go box, and we'll go."

Her face serene, Patrea demurred. "No. We'll stay." She turned her eyes away from where he sat, and studiously avoided looking at him directly. He made no such effort, and though it was pinned on her, even I could feel the heat of his gaze. Talk about sexual tension.

Miranda commented on it when she brought our wings. "I've never seen Chris look at anyone like that. You're a lucky woman."

"If she only knew." Snorting, Patrea doused the fries with malt vinegar and a hail of salt, then selected the longest one on the plate. Slowly, she took a bite, arched her neck, closed her eyes, and made yummy noises. Not, I thought, because the fries were so good—they were, but the show was strictly for Chris Evergreen's benefit.

"You know, I almost pity that poor man."

Patrea started to say something, but trailed off, her eyes widening. I turned to see why, and mine nearly fell out of my head.

"You can see her?" Wearing the same outfit from the photos we'd looked at earlier, her hair in the same, loose style, the ghost of Amber Hale sat on the barstool next to Chris.

"Of course, I can see her. What is wrong with you?"

I looked again, and this time, I caught the subtle differences. The presumed-missing Mia James was no longer missing.

"Okay, that's just creepy."

"You think?" I slid my chair around a little so I could have a better view, and I didn't care if Mia noticed the change or not. I didn't have to worry, with her attention focused on Chris, she wouldn't have noticed a purple elephant with a pink cotton bunny tail dancing on a rainbow with a unicorn.

When her hand fell on his forearm, he finally turned to look at her, and I saw the sudden stiffness of his shock. Mia fiddled with the locket at her neck, tilted her head, and said something that had him shaking his head.

"Oh, she didn't like that one bit." Patrea smirked. Mia's face flushed an unbecoming shade. She looked more like herself when she glowered. "Time to let him off the hook."

I watched Chris while he watched Patrea stand and walk slowly toward him. His chest hitched, but he kept his face passive. Good, I thought, make her work for it a little, she'll appreciate you more.

For all the stupid comments she made about her romance quotient, Patrea was due for a meal of crow. No Hallmark couple ever had this much chemistry. He stood to meet her, and when the two melted into each other, I wanted to cheer.

Mia did not share my enthusiasm. Fury rode her features like a thundercloud hugs the sky. Fists clenched, she angled her body to avoid touching the fused-together couple, and headed toward the restrooms. Instead of passing, she stopped at my table, leaned over and rested her hands on the edge so her face was close to mine.

"Your friend will pay for coming between me and what I want. You'll pay, too. By the time I'm done smearing your name, no one will believe the sky is blue on your say so."

Maybe she could pull that off, and maybe not, but when she'd leaned over, I got a good look at the locket hanging around her neck.

"That's mine," Amber screeched in my ear loud enough to make me cringe, and Mia thought she'd scored.

"That's right, you should be scared. Your life, as you know it, is over."

"The hell it is." Pure rage fueled Amber's energy. Without thinking, she reached for the platter of wings, and slammed it into Mia's face once.

"That's for stealing my Momma's necklace."

Twice.

"That's for threatening my friend."

Three times.

"And that's for killing me."

Mia's eyes rolled back in her head, and she went down with a thud.

"Hey," Amber grinned. "Why didn't you tell me I could do that?"

181

The commotion had drawn too much attention for me to be able to answer.

"Are you all right?" Miranda came around the end of the bar. "What happened?"

"Call Ernie Polk. Tell him to hurry." As Miranda turned to do as I'd asked, I grabbed the bar cloth she'd tucked into the waistband of her apron, and twisted it into a makeshift rope.

"What the hell?" Patrea might not have seen what happened, but she pitched right in when I asked her to help me tie Mia's hands behind her back.

"Don't touch that locket, it probably still has Amber's prints on it somewhere."

As it turned out, Amber's prints were on the locket, but Ernie didn't need them. Mia confessed—at the top of her lungs, no less—to the murder of Amber, and she admitted she'd roofied Lance Colby. Anything Amber had, Mia wanted, and that included the cameraman in her bed.

She'd slipped another into Chris's beer right there at the bar, too.

Ernie hauled Mia off to jail, and after making plans to spend Christmas Eve with Chris, Patrea came home with me. This was the first time I'd collared a killer without ending up nearly dying myself. Chalk that up in the win column.

"I'm sorry." Patrea's comment came out of nowhere as we sat at the kitchen table unwinding from a whopper of a day. With Molly snuggled warmly against my feet, a cup of hot chocolate loaded with marshmallows, and Christmas nearly upon me, I felt pretty good.

"Sorry for what?"

"That I thought you were an idiot and running away from your problems when you moved back here."

"Why thanks, I guess."

Sure, there was still the stuff with Paul and his family hanging over my head, but I didn't think any of the local news stations would be sending out more reporters after what had happened to Amber and Mia. I had Patrea to help me with the legal stuff, and my house was newly ghost-free. Life was good.

"That didn't sound exactly the way I meant it, but now I see you were running to something, and not away. You've got a great life here, though I guess I should probably tell you something."

From her tone, it didn't sound like good news was coming my way. "Hit me, I can take it." I took a sip of my hot chocolate.

"I really do hate to say it, but your house is haunted."

I spit a little of my drink. "What makes you say that?"

"Cold spots mostly, and every so often, I swear I can hear someone talking. Just faintly."

"She's not wrong," Amber shattered my illusions. "Your house is haunted, and I'm not ready to leave."

Great. Well, two out of three wasn't bad, and I'd find a way to talk Amber into going.

"If there's a ghost here, I can live with that." It was time to change the subject. "Looks like you got the full small-town Christmas movie experience. Romance, mystery, plenty of holiday cheer. There's only one thing left to do."

"What would that be?" In her candy cane jammies, and with the glow of Chris still on her face, Patrea looked young and happy.

"I want to give you your Christmas present."

"Right now?" It was late, well past midnight, but I didn't want to wait, and it wasn't like either of us would get to sleep anytime soon.

"Right now. Come on." I'd already taken the key out of the drawer. "It's time to show you Catherine's secret." I unlocked the door to the addition and wondered if there was anything I could say to prepare Patrea for the jumble she'd find on the other side. Nothing came to mind, so I opened the door, hit the lights and stepped aside to give her the full impact.

The sight rendered her speechless. For about a half a minute anyway. "This is nuts."

"With the exception of the painting on the easel in the loft, you're free to choose anything you want from in here."

"Anything?"

"Anything."

Eyes shining, Patrea exclaimed, "Eat your heart out, Hallmark!"

CPSIA information can be obtained
at www.ICGtesting.com
Printed in the USA
BVHW031029111020
590782BV00001B/125